THE JUDGEMENT OF LOVE

From the library of

Name________________________

Address________________________

THE ROMANTIC NOVELS OF

BARBARA CARTLAND

THE JUDGEMENT OF LOVE

Eaglemoss Publications Limited,
7 Cromwell Road,
London SW7 2HR

First published Hutchinson hardback 1979
Hutchinson paperbacks (Arrow Books) 1980
This edition Eaglemoss Publications 1986

Set in Sabon
Made and printed in Great Britain by
Richard Clay Ltd,
Bungay, Suffolk

ISBN 1 85167 203 6

THE JUDGEMENT OF LOVE

'Perhaps I am asking too much, to expect the same love that Papa and Mama had for each other,' Astara thought now.

But she knew what she was seeking was a love which was somehow linked with the beauty which lay in front of her – the shimmer of silver on the lake, the purple shadows beneath the trees, the mystery of the garden which she felt might be peopled by the ghosts of those who had lived here in the past.

"What is love? Is it part of beauty? Is it what Papa tried to describe to me as 'the world beyond the world'?"

She asked the questions and did not know the answers. Then she realised she was cold.

'Perhaps one day I shall find out,' she thought, looking up at the moon.

Then shivering a little she pulled the curtains to and climbed into the darkness of the big silk-canopied bed.

AUTHOR'S NOTE

Many famous artists have painted "The Judgement of Paris", but I personally find the one by Johann Van Aachen is the most beautiful of them all. It is now in the Musée de la Chartreuse at Douai in France.

Johann Van Aachen was born in Cologne in 1552 when the golden age of German painting was nearly over. He studied in Italy the works of Tintoretto and Michelangelo.

On his return he was appointed Court Painter to Emperor Rudolf II. A brilliant technician, his colour and style is very inspiring. He died in Prague in 1615.

The Association for Promoting the Discovery of the Interior Part of Africa was founded in London in 1788 and later merged in 1830 with the Royal Geographical Society. The *Société de Géographes* was founded in Paris in 1821.

CHAPTER ONE

1820

"This is a perfect room for your pictures!" Astara exclaimed.

"That is what I thought you would think," Sir Roderick replied.

Astara looked around her with delight at the huge Georgian Salon.

It had white walls, a heavily gilded cornice and three windows opening out onto a terrace which led down to the garden.

The pale April sunshine coming into the room rested on damask-covered French furniture and an Aubusson carpet with a riot of cupids and flowers.

It might, Sir Roderick thought, looking at her, have been designed as a frame for Astara herself.

In all the long years of his life he had never seen anything quite so exquisite as her fair hair which at times seemed almost to have a touch of fire in it and framed her heart-shaped face.

Her blue eyes were the colour of a stormy Mediterranean sea, her skin like the petals of a magnolia blossom.

When she was fifteen he had left her, after her parents' death, at a School in Florence and had expected that she would grow into a beauty.

But when he had returned two years later it was to find that she had exceeded all his expectations.

Now with an enthusiasm and a sparkling vitality which Sir Roderick found irresistible Astara clapped her hands.

"I have found it!" she exclaimed. "Found the ideal spot for our picture."

"Which one?" Sir Roderick enquired. "We have, if you remember, collected over a hundred!"

"You know exactly the one I mean," Astara said, "and it would look perfect over that carved marble mantelpiece!"

"I presume," he said teasing her, "that you mean 'The Judgement of Paris' by a comparatively unknown German artist?"

"Of course I mean 'The Judgement of Paris'," she replied. "It is the loveliest painting I have ever seen and I would sacrifice all your Cranachs, Guardis and Poussins to possess it!"

"I only hope that some great Art Connoisseur does not hear you," Sir Roderick replied dryly. "Though I grant you Johann Van Aachen has done a very good job with this painting, which shows perhaps more than any of his other paintings that he studied the styles of Tintoretto and Michelangelo."

He realised as he spoke that Astara was not listening to him.

She was staring at the mantelpiece and the space over it from which Sir Roderick had ordered the removal of one of the Woottons which his father had collected so arduously.

It had not been the right place for a sporting picture, though Sir Roderick knew it was an exceptionally fine one.

He had already decided that the paintings by Wootton, Stubbs and Hondecoeter should all be rehung in the Hall and in his Library.

There was a great deal to do to Worfield Park, but on his way back to England he had looked forward to redecorating the great house with the help of Astara.

He knew that the time she had spent in Florence had given her an education very different from that enjoyed by most English girls, and he had learnt when they were in Rome how knowledgeable she was on sculpture and the ancient Temples with which Rome abounded.

She was like a goddess herself, he thought, as she moved across the room to link her arm into his and say beguilingly:

"What fun we are going to have, Uncle Roderick. I have not had a home for so many years that everything about yours fascinates me."

"I thought it would," Sir Roderick said, "and I am only wondering how long you will stay with me so that we can enjoy it together."

She looked at him with a surprised expression in her eyes and he explained:

"Judging by the number of young men in Rome who cast their hearts, their titles and their dilapidated Palaces at your feet, I cannot help anticipating that the same thing will happen in England."

Astara gave a little laugh and two dimples appeared in her cheeks.

"Dilapidated is the right word for most of the Palaces!" she replied, "and I have a suspicion that a great deal of their eagerness to marry me was due to the very large dowry they expected you would give me."

"You can say the same thing of the noblemen who pursued you in Paris!"

"The French are very shrewd when it comes to business," Astara replied demurely.

Sir Roderick laughed.

"As it happens I have every intention that you shall marry an Englishman. I want you to live here one day and I would like to think that when I am dead your children will be playing on the lawns and sliding along the Picture Gallery."

"Do not talk of dying," Astara begged. "That is something that will not happen for many, many years, and you know it would break my . . heart to . . lose you. You are all the . . family I have."

There was a little break in her voice which told Sir Roderick that she still missed her mother and father almost unbearably.

Looking back at when he had last seen the three of them together he had thought that he had never known people so happy.

But then Astara's father and mother had loved each other in a way that few men and women are privileged to love.

Because they had died together there had been no disillusionment and no broken-hearted widow or widower left behind.

There had only been Astara, and when he had received her cry for help he had gladly gone to her, knowing that he would devote what years were left to him to looking after and caring for her.

He had often wondered if his closest friend who was Charles Beverley, although he was a much younger man, had had a strange premonition that he and his beloved wife would not return from the journey of exploration they were to make amongst the mountains of Turkey.

While they were there, there had been a violent earthquake and no-one in the vicinity had lived to relate exactly what had happened.

They had provided for Astara in what was the most sensible manner possible by making her a Ward of Sir Roderick Worfield. They loved him and he was as it happened an extremely rich man.

He himself had never married.

He had been too busy when he was young in making a great fortune, and in fact the only woman he had ever loved and wished to make his wife had fallen in love with Charles Beverley, and he with her, at first sight.

A man of less fine character than Sir Roderick might have been jealous and resented that he had brought together the two people he cared for most in the world, only in one way to lose them both.

From the moment they met Charles and Charlotte

Beverley ceased to remember that anyone else existed in the whole world.

Charles had always been a traveller and in an amateur way an explorer.

Charlotte would have been perfectly happy to explore the moon if he had asked it of her.

Sir Roderick often thought it was quite incidental that they had a daughter. They both adored Astara who merely added to their happiness and they never found her an encumbrance for the simple reason that they never let her become one.

When they went travelling they took her with them.

By the time Astara was ten years old she had travelled in a *dhow* down the Nile, she had been capsized from a canoe in a crocodile-infested river, and she had encountered so many storms at sea that inevitably she had become a good sailor.

And she had seen parts of the world into which few adults, let alone children, had ever penetrated.

She was, not surprisingly, by the time she came under the care of Sir Roderick, extremely intelligent and knowledgeable about many subjects of which another girl of her age would have been completely ignorant.

Sir Roderick thought what she needed was a sophisticated polish which would enable her to take her place in Society and ensure that her unusual and unique beauty acquired the right frame.

Sir Roderick was very much a man of the world and because he was so rich there was not a Capital in which he was not welcomed or a house in any country where its owner was not proud to entertain him.

The Worfields were an old and distinguished family and Sir Roderick was the seventh Baronet.

It would have been quite easy for him, since so many countries asked his advice and found they profited by it, to have acquired a number of other important titles, but he was not interested.

He was, however, extremely proud of the large and

magnificent Mansion in Hertfordshire that had been in the Worfield family for nearly five hundred years.

His grandfather had added to it and the main part had been completely rebuilt by Robert Adam.

It was these rooms which Sir Roderick thought were particularly right for Astara and he had spent the last two years when they were travelling about Europe acquiring pictures and other treasures with which to embellish them.

It had amused Sir Roderick when Astara was captivated in Paris by a picture by Johann Van Aachen who, a brilliant technician, had been Court painter to the exacting Emperor Rudolf II.

He could understand Astara's enthusiasm for "The Judgement of Paris" because she herself resembled very closely the three lovely, ethereal goddesses who stood in front of the handsome young Trojan, each one confident she would receive the golden apple he would give to the most beautiful of them.

There was something about Astara, Sir Roderick thought, that was different from any other woman he had ever met.

It was something ethereal and difficult to put into words, and yet he knew it was this which made men fall head-over-heels in love with her the moment they saw her.

It also told him that London would be no different from Rome or Paris and he would spend most of his time fending off the fortune-hunters.

He made no secret of the fact that he considered Astara his adopted daughter and that she would inherit a great deal, if not all, of his fortune.

It suddenly struck him as he walked across the room and out into the Hall where a number of servants were unpacking the huge cases in which the purchases they had made in Europe had travelled with them to England, that it might eventually prove more of a curse than a blessing.

Sir Roderick called to his Agent who was supervising the operations.

"I want two men, Mr. Barnes, to bring that picture over there into the Salon and hold it up over the mantelpiece."

"Certainly, Sir Roderick," Mr. Barnes answered.

He followed the direction in which Sir Roderick pointed and he ordered two footmen to carry the picture into the Salon.

It was quite large and its frame was gilded and heavily carved. As they held it up Sir Roderick knew that Astara's good taste was uneering.

"It is perfect, just as I knew it would be!" she cried. "It picks up the pinks in the carpet, the blue of the ceiling and I feel as if the whole room revolves around it."

"Then it shall be hung at once!" Sir Roderick smiled, and gave the order.

They decided the position of several other paintings. Then Sir Roderick suggested it would be best to get most of them up on the walls so that they could sort them out later and arrange them to their best advantage.

"There are so many other things I wish to show you, my dearest child," he said to Astara, "that our new acquisitions will have to wait their turn."

She smiled with delight for already she was finding that England had attractions she had not found in any other country.

She had not been in England for eight years and she had almost forgotten, she told Sir Roderick, how beautiful it was.

The daffodils made a carpet of gold in the Park and there were primroses in the hedgerows as they drove from London, and in the garden the first shrubs were coming into bud.

"It is even lovelier than I imagined it would be!" she said excitedly, "and I really feel as if I have come home."

Sir Roderick was delighted, as she knew he would be.

That evening as they sat in the Salon after dinner and

he saw that her eyes continually wandered to the picture over the mantelpiece, he said:

"Your appreciation for 'The Judgement of Paris' has given me an idea!"

"What is that?" Astara enquired.

"I want you to sit in judgement not on three beautiful women, but on three handsome men!"

She looked at him in surprise and he went on:

"I have already told you that when I am dead you will inherit my fortune, but as you are aware there are always penalties attached to great wealth especially where a woman is concerned."

He spoke seriously and Astara slipped from the sofa on which she had been sitting to kneel beside his chair.

"Then do not give me so much," she said. "I know that you are afraid of my being pursued by fortune-hunters, and I feel it is a mistake to put temptation in their way."

"It is certainly a case of gilding the lily," Sir Roderick agreed. "You are so lovely, my dearest, that any man would love you if you were the proverbial 'beggar maiden', but we are both sensible enough to realise that most men find wealth irresistible."

"I want to be . . loved for . . myself," Astara said in a low voice.

"And you will be, that I promise you," Sir Roderick replied. "No-one who knew you could not love you, but I wish to ensure that when I am no longer here my money is handled in the right way."

Astara did not speak and after a moment he said:

"You know as well as I do that the Law gives a man complete and absolute control over his wife's fortune. Therefore, what we have to find is a man whom you will not only love, but respect and trust."

"Do you think that will be difficult?"

"Not if you allow me to suggest three applicants for your hand in whom I have complete confidence."

Astara was still for a moment, then she said:

"You would not . . force me to . . marry anyone I did not . . love?"

"I want you to find the same happiness that your father and mother knew," Sir Roderick replied, "and it would have been impossible not to love your mother."

There was a note in his voice which Astara understood and she said gently:

"You loved Mama very deeply, did you not?"

"I never loved anyone else," Sir Roderick answered, "and that is why, whatever sort of girl you were, you were your mother's daughter and I was prepared to devote my whole life to you."

He put his hand on Astara's golden head before he said:

"But you know now that I love you for yourself and I have to try to find a man who will care for you as I do, and also protect you."

"Who are you . . suggesting?" Astara asked in a low voice.

"My three nephews," Sir Roderick replied.

"Your three nephews?" Astara repeated. "I suppose it is very stupid of me and perhaps rather rude, but I have never asked you about your family. I have always thought of you somehow as being alone."

"That is exactly what I always have been," Sir Roderick said. "I like my independence. I have enjoyed moving about the world with no ties, concentrating on business and, as you know, most profitably."

He smiled as if pleased with his own success. Then he went on:

"But I do have relations and amongst them are three young men who are Worfields and could, therefore, be trusted with my greatest and most valuable treasure – which is you!"

Astara laid her head against his knee.

"You are making me depressed," she protested, "because you will keep talking about leaving me. I am so happy with you, Uncle Roderick, that I have no wish to be married."

"You are nineteen," Sir Roderick replied, "and I cannot allow you to *coiffer Sainte Catherine*."

Astara knew that this meant to become an Old Maid in French and she laughed.

"I do not think it is likely," Sir Roderick went on before she could speak, "but there is no harm in taking precautions. So before I take you to London, where you will undoubtedly be the instantaneous success you have been in Paris and Rome, I want you to meet my three nephews."

"Of course I will meet them," Astara agreed, "but must I hand one of them an apple, and a very golden one at that?"

"We will leave the final result of your judgement in the hands of destiny," Sir Roderick replied, "but it will amuse me to see the response from my nephews to the letter which I intend to write to them."

"Tell me about them first," Astara pleaded. "You are making me nervous."

"There is no reason to be," Sir Roderick answered, "and you must pander to an old man's whims, although we may find that on this we do not eventually see eye to eye."

"Once again I must ask you to promise me," Astara pleaded, "that I do not have to . . marry any man unless I can give him my . . heart."

"That I promise you," Sir Roderick said, "but perhaps I am being prophetic in that I am quite certain you will find in one of my nephews, who are all extremely handsome, the man whom fate intended you to have as your mate."

Astara was silent and because he knew she was waiting to hear more he said:

"You will have seen in his portraits that my father was an exceedingly handsome man."

"As you are!" Astara said quickly.

"I was reasonably good-looking when I was young," Sir Roderick admitted, "and there were quite a number of lovely ladies to tell me so. But my three younger brothers were equally good-looking. In fact we commanded quite a lot of attention wherever we went."

"I wish I had known you then," Astara said. "Then

instead of wanting to marry Mama you could have married me!"

Sir Roderick touched her cheek in a loving gesture before he continued:

"I think it must have been some past ancestor who inspired us with desire to succeed with an ambition which was almost insatiable."

"Was it ambition that made you work to acquire such a large fortune?" Astara asked.

"Of course!" Sir Roderick replied, "I was ambitious to prove myself; to show that my brain was better than other men's."

He gave a little chuckle as he said:

"Every time I brought off a big financial coup I felt I was like a peacock spreading my tail to proclaim my own cleverness!"

Astara looked up at him and laughed.

"I can understand exactly what you felt. It must have been fun . . great fun!"

"My brothers were inspired in the same way," Sir Roderick told her. "George who is only a year younger than I went into politics, moved from the Commons to the House of Lords and was created Earl of Yeldham when he was appointed Lord Lieutenant of Ireland."

"He was certainly successful!" Astara exclaimed.

"His son," Sir Roderick said, "is the Viscount Yelverton, and William has already distinguished himself amongst the Bucks and Beaux of St. James's."

Astara waited, her eyes on Sir Roderick's face.

"William," he said slowly, "is a Corinthian and outstanding in every field of sport. I do not need to tell you that he is exceedingly handsome and there is no bachelor, I believe, more sought after by the great Whig hostesses."

He looked at Astara fondly as he added:

"As William's wife you would take your place in the Social World as a Queen, and I cannot imagine any two people who would, in appearance, seem more obviously to have been made for each other."

Astara looked up at the picture above them.

"Paris had three goddesses to choose from," she said. "Having offered me Apollo . . who next?"

"My brother Mark, Lord Worfield, is at the moment Lord Chancellor of England," Sir Roderick replied.

"He has certainly achieved his ambition!" Astara exclaimed. "I believe there is no higher position in any Government with the exception of Prime Minister."

"I am quite certain that Mark bows his head only to the King," Sir Roderick answered. "He was always very studious as a young man, but he had the gift of oratory and that has certainly carried him to great heights."

"And his son?"

"His son, Lionel, is a soldier and I believe both efficient and gallant. He will, I suppose, be about twenty-six so he was very young when he had the chance of proving himself on the battlefield, and he was decorated by the Duke of Wellington himself!"

"And he is also handsome?" Astara asked.

"I am told that in uniform he makes every woman's heart beat faster and the King, when he was Prince Regent, wished always to be attended by the most distinguished and handsome Bucks and continually asked him and William to Carlton House."

"You paint a most alluring picture," Astara said. "It is a pity that it has to be in words and not in oils."

"Portraits are usually extremely deceptive," Sir Roderick said, "and that reminds me, I wish to have you painted. The difficulty will be to decide which English artist will really do you justice."

"I have no wish to sit for hours when I can be out riding with you, or dancing with the handsome William!"

She gave a little cry.

"Uncle Roderick, we must give a Ball! Think what fun it would be! And you know in Paris you danced so much better than any of the young men who partnered me."

"Again you are flattering me!" Sir Roderick smiled, "but

a Ball is certainly an idea, and as it happens, I already intended not only to give a Ball here, but also in London."

He saw the delight in Astara's eyes. Then added:

"But I would like your 'judgement' to come first."

There was a little silence. Then Astara said:

"You are .. apprehensive about my appearing in London! Why?"

"You know that because you are particularly astute," Sir Roderick answered, "but it is true. I am slightly apprehensive."

"Tell me why you should be so?" Astara begged.

"I do not know whether you have heard about the looseness of morals in English Society to-day," Sir Roderick replied, "but it is something that is talked about frequently on the Continent."

"They certainly talked about the Prince Regent!" Astara agreed.

"Then you will realise," Sir Roderick said, "that since the late King, poor man, was completely mad, he led the Social World and people took their standards from him."

He paused before he continued:

"His love-affairs all through his life as Prince of Wales have set a bad example, while his disastrous marriage and the fact that he is now besotted by Lady Conyngham makes the *Beau Monde* not the best of places in which to present someone like yourself."

"Why should I be different?" Astara asked.

"If you want me to tell you the truth," Sir Roderick replied, "it is because you are not only beautiful, my dearest, but also pure and, I think where men are concerned, innocent."

He saw the flush that came to her cheeks.

"Perhaps I am being presumptuous," he went on, "and if I am you must forgive me, but I would like to know if you have ever been kissed?"

"No, of course not!" Astara said quickly.

Then as she felt he was waiting for an explanation she added:

"To be truthful, Uncle Roderick, I have never met anyone I really wanted to kiss me. Quite a number of men have tried, but I have always felt a kiss was something so . . intimate that I would give my . . lips only to the man I . . loved."

There was something very moving in Astara's soft voice and Sir Roderick said with a note of triumph in his voice:

"That is exactly what I thought you would feel, and that is why I would like you to be married, or at least engaged, before I can take you to London."

"You are really afraid of what . . might happen to me?"

"A rough wind can blow the petals from a flower," Sir Roderick answered, "and I also have a violent dislike of the thought of you being toasted as an 'Incomparable', which undoubtedly you are, by the drunken Fops who congregate in the Clubs in St. James's."

"You may have heard one thing about London and I have heard another," Astara said after a moment, "but just as you have shown me Rome and Paris, I would not like to be ignorant of my own country."

She clasped her hands together before she went on:

"I am English and you are English too. We may not approve of everything we see and hear, but whatever it is like, it is part of ourselves."

"You are right," Sir Roderick agreed. "Of course you are right! But I still ask you to bear with me and meet my nephews before we go to London."

"You know I will do anything you ask of me," Astara replied. "How could I refuse you when you have been so kind and I love you?"

"Then we are agreed," Sir Roderick said, "and tomorrow, to save my old eyes, I will get you to write three letters for me which I assure you will bring my nephews here as quickly as a horse can carry them!"

"You have told me about two of your nephews," Astara said, as if she had suddenly thought of it, "but you have not mentioned the third. Paris had to judge between three goddesses."

"I have three nephews as I had three brothers," Sir Roderick said, "but the third need hardly concern us."

"Why not?"

"Because my youngest brother Luke was a failure."

"I thought you were all successful."

"All except one," Sir Roderick said, "and he was a great disappointment to my father."

"What did he do?" Astara asked curiously.

"It was traditional as in most big families," Sir Roderick replied, "that while the eldest son devoted himself to the estate, the second would go into politics, the third into the Army, and the fourth into the Church."

"And did your younger brother refuse?"

"No. Luke accepted," Sir Roderick replied, "and he had the choice of fifteen parishes which were in my father's gift."

Astara was listening intently as Sir Roderick went on:

"Some were, of course, better endowed and more important than others, but Luke chose a very small Parish near here, and even before he was ordained he got married."

"Was your father annoyed?"

"Naturally," Sir Roderick replied. "He considered Luke far too young to know his own mind and what is more he had chosen someone quite unimportant with nothing to recommend her except that she was extremely pretty."

Astara waited.

"My father determined, however, that unsatisfactory as Luke might appear, he must not let the family down. If he became a Bishop, then he could hold up his head with his brothers, and the hasty mesalliance of his marriage would be forgotten."

"I can almost guess the end of the story," Astara smiled.

Sir Roderick shook his head.

"Luke was a great disappointment. He refused every chance of promotion that was offered him and there was a great many. He refused to leave Little Milden and remained there until his death."

Sir Roderick's voice was scathing as he continued:

"They tell me that he was adored in the neighbourhood but that did not placate my father who wished him to operate in a very much larger field than Little Milden could supply."

"And what about his son?" Astara asked.

"Vulcan is, I regret to say, as difficult as his father."

"Vulcan? What a strange name!"

"Extremely strange, as you can imagine, for the son of a parson," Sir Roderick retorted. "In fact the boy, my father's first grandchild, was christened before he could interfere. He was absolutely livid when he heard the name he had been given."

"Vulcan was the god of the thunderbolt," Astara said reflectively, "as the god of Fire and family he became thought of as the origin of life-giving warmth."

"You certainly have a retentive memory," Sir Roderick said dryly, "but I doubt if my nephew Vulcan is any of those things."

"What does he do?" Astara enquired.

"He is now nearly thirty and has spent many of those years climbing mountains, moving about the world, usually I believe, on foot or on the back of a mule."

"Papa would have considered that commendable and adventurous!" Astara exclaimed.

"Your father was different!" Sir Roderick retorted "From all I hear Vulcan has just been a wanderer, enjoying himself in strange, outlandish places without a thought of using his talents."

"Nevertheless, he is number three in your trio. But suppose it is impossible to get hold of him?"

"As a matter of fact I have already learnt from Barnes after my brother's death he converted the dilapidated Mill at Little Milden into a home for himself. When he is in England that is where he lives."

"And you think he is there now?"

"Barnes tells me he is definitely there, so he can be invited here as well as William and Lionel."

"I have a feeling that you favour William."

"I am trying to be impartial," Sir Roderick replied, "and leave the award entirely to you."

"But you cannot help pushing your favourite!" she smiled.

"I suppose really I feel rather envious of the young men who are acclaimed Corinthians, who can drive a Phaeton with an expertise that I never had time to acquire, and who are undoubtedly extremely adept at flooring bullies with their fists or duelling with their equals."

Astara laughed in sheer delight.

"Uncle Roderick, you should write a book! You describe things so much more vividly than any of those prosy volumes I have read in English. The French do it much better."

"But French Literature is something I do not always recommend for someone as young as you," Sir Roderick said quickly.

"You are trying too hard to protect me not from other people, but from myself," Astara said. "You see, most beloved of uncles, I have to grow up. I have to learn to make decisions and even to make my own mistakes."

She looked so lovely as she spoke in a serious way that Sir Roderick bent forward to put his arm round her shoulders.

"God knows I want to protect you," he said, "and I know, perhaps better than most people, that this can be a difficult and sometimes frightening world for a young woman who is alone."

"But I am not alone," Astara protested. "I have you."

"You know that I am over seventy," Sir Roderick answered, "and I have to think of your future. Help me, my dearest, to do what is right – for no man knows how long his life will last."

He knew as he spoke that such an appeal would receive an instant response from Astara's warm heart.

She took his hand and pressed it against her cheek.

"You know I will do anything you ask of me," she said. "We will write to your three nephews and I hope that when I have met them I shall be able to give you your heart's desire and say that one of them, perhaps William, is the man I wish to marry."

"It would be impossible for them not to fall in love with you," Sir Roderick said, "and the Worfields, especially my brothers and myself, have always been very careful and sensible where money is concerned."

He paused before he continued:

"Our father was a rich man, and he was also very just in that he gave us quite early in life, what money he could afford. I remember him saying very solemnly: 'You all know the parable in the Bible of the Talents. I can only recommend you all to read it and remember that the servant who hid his one talent in the ground was rebuked for being wicked and slothful!' "

"You certainly did not do that!"

"I had intelligence and the ability to see that my talents multiplied a thousandfold," Sir Roderick said. "George, the Earl of Yeldham, certainly made use of his, and so did Mark, now Lord Worfield, the title to which his son Lionel will succeed on his death."

"They both sound very attractive," Astara remarked, "and I am sorry for Vulcan, for what has he inherited?"

"Only a wanderlust and an old Mill!" Sir Roderick said dramatically, and they both laughed.

Later that night when Astara was in the Bed-Room that she knew had been specially chosen for her by her uncle because it was the most elaborate and attractive in the house, she stood at the window looking out at the moonlight.

It had rained earlier in the evening and everything smelt with the freshness that she had forgotten was a part of England.

By the light of the moon she could see the great trees in the Park which had stood there for generations, and below the house was a lake fed by a stream which meandered away between green fields.

There was a stone bridge from under which she had seen in the daytime swans emerging like ships with full-bellied sails moving before the wind.

It was all so peaceful that she knew her uncle was right and that one day she would like to live here and bring up a family.

And yet, at the same time something within her made her long to see and discover more of the world.

It was a feeling which she knew had driven her father into far-off lands and was in fact responsible for her name.

Astara was a town on the shore of the Caspian Sea.

Charles Beverley had been travelling in Persia when one day he had looked across the blue expanse of water and told himself it had a strange, compelling beauty that aroused him in a manner he found it hard to explain.

"I only knew," he said to Astara when she was old enough to understand, "that it evoked in me a feeling which I have never forgotten."

He paused before he went on:

"There are places that lift one's spirit and inspire one. Most as far as I am concerned have been strange and unexpected and not those that are written up in the Guide Books."

He saw that Astara was listening and trying to understand, and he went on almost as if he was speaking to himself:

"It is in those moments that our spirits, or perhaps you would say our souls, touch the infinite and we pass out of this world and into another that as yet, we cannot understand."

"Like going to Heaven, Papa?" Astara had asked.

"Men have many names for the Divine," her father replied. "They call it Heaven or Paradise, Nivanah or Valhalla, and there are many others. But what it all comes down to is that man is naturally and perceptively aware that there is another world besides this one."

"I . . think I . . understand," Astara said.

"You will understand when you know the feeling I have tried to describe, when you step if only for a split second into the world beyond this one: a world of inexpressible beauty."

There was something almost ecstatic in her father's voice and Astara had watched the expression on his face for some time before she said:

"I shall try, Papa, to find the world you describe to me."

"You will find it!" her father said positively, "of that I am sure!"

Astara had never forgotten that conversation and now she thought that it was this search for beauty that had driven her father and mother to travel so extensively.

She wished she had been old enough to remember everything that had happened while she was with them.

But she thought now that each one of their journeys had been a voyage of discovery, and because of what she had learnt she must go on as they had done looking for the world beyond the world.

Whether it was in some far off mountain range, an unmapped river or perhaps here at home beside the lake and under the oak trees in the Park was immaterial!

It was not time or place that mattered, Astara knew, but what one felt in the secret shrine within one's self which held the soul.

This was the sort of thing, she thought, that she had never been able to talk about with anyone, not even with her closest friend at School or now with her Guardian whom she called "Uncle Roderick".

She loved him, she loved the sharpness of his brain, the compassion and understanding which he showed in every word he spoke to her.

But these other things which had been planted in her mind by her father were not anything she could put into words or explain except to herself.

'Perhaps one day,' she thought, 'I will find a man who will understand.'

Then she was afraid she was being optimistic.

The men she had met in Rome and in Paris had been in love with her but, innocent though she was, she knew that it was her body that interested them, not her mind or her soul.

She would have found it embarrassing, as they would

have, to speak to them of such things.

They wanted her because she was beautiful.

"I love you!" "You drive me mad!" "Can you not understand if you will not marry me the only thing left for me is to die?" "I want you!" "I want you!"

She could hear their voices repeating more or less the same words but always with the same intensity of feeling.

The Italians were perhaps the most eloquent and she had found the fire flashing in their dark eyes was exciting, except sometimes when they became over-dramatic and made her want to laugh.

The Frenchmen had been more subtle.

They paid her the sort of compliments it was impossible for her not to appreciate. They had such exquisite manners, and many of them were very graceful.

But although she listened to them with her ears she found that nothing stirred in her heart.

When they covered her hands with kisses she only found herself thinking that their lips were hot and far too possessive, and vaguely she felt slightly repulsed because it was all so theatrical and un-real.

'Perhaps I am asking too much, to expect the same love that Papa and Mama had for each other,' Astara thought now.

But she knew that what she was seeking was a love which was somehow linked with the beauty which lay in front of her – the shimmer of silver on the lake, the purple shadows beneath the trees, the mystery of the garden which she felt might be peopled by the ghosts of those who had lived here in the past.

"What is love? Is it part of beauty? Is it what Papa tried to describe to me as 'the world beyond the world'?"

She asked the questions and did not know the answers. Then she realised she was cold.

'Perhaps one day I shall find out,' she thought looking up at the moon.

Then shivering a little she pulled the curtains to and climbed into the darkness of the big silk-canopied bed.

CHAPTER TWO

King George IV rose to his feet. He stood for a moment waiting for silence from the nineteen gentlemen seated round the Dining-Room table.

Somehow, against a background of walls papered with silver and the columns of red and yellow granite, the gentlemen still managed to look highly decorative.

The long table with its enormous gold ornamentations and blue Sèvres china was sensational in that the King had introduced the fashion of not using a white linen cloth.

Instead on its polished surface the crystal goblets embellished with his monogram, the gold dessert knives and forks, and the Waterford glass decanters were reflected as if by a mirror.

As every face at the table was turned towards him His Majesty raised his glass.

"Gentlemen," he said, "I give you a toast–to an outstanding thoroughbred which gave us to-day a race that will long be remembered in the history of the turf – Topsail, and his popular owner Viscount Yelverton!"

The guests rose to their feet with the exception of the Viscount who was sitting at the end of the table.

Glasses were raised and nineteen voices cried:

"Topsail! Yelverton!"

As the King seated himself and his guests followed him the Viscount got up.

There was no doubt he looked extremely elegant and distinguished. There was not a man present who did not glance appreciatively at the manner in which he had tied his cravat in a style they had not seen before.

Speaking in a low but carrying voice and showing that he was an accomplished orator as well as having so many other outstanding qualities, the Viscount said:

"May I thank Your Majesty and you, my friends, for your appreciation of my horse? I feel you would all like me to say that, if any of us have successes on the turf such as I have enjoyed this afternoon, it is because this 'Sport of Kings' has been encouraged, supported and, if I may say the word, inspired by the greatest sportsman of us all – the King!"

Everybody jumped up to drink the King's health and there was no doubt that he was delighted at the compliment and the manner in which the Viscount had turned the tribute from himself into one to his host.

It was in fact true that the King's chief delight was the turf, to which he had been introduced by the Duke of Cumberland.

Indeed, when he was young, one of the grooms at Carlton House had remarked that horses were the one and only subject of his thoughts.

He went racing whenever he could and regularly attended Lewes, Brighton and Newmarket Races.

But like everything else the King loved, his racing had its ups and downs.

At the end of the century his stud had been broken up in accordance with his proclaimed intention of leading a more economical life, but he had quickly built up a new racing establishment at Newmarket and in eleven years his horses had won no less than 1,185 races.

Newmarket, however, was later "taboo" owing to a scandal over his jockey Samuel Chiffney, and to the dismay and concern of many of his friends the King declared he would have no more to do with Newmarket.

This did not prevent him from attending all other race-meetings and spending far more money on the horses than he could possibly afford.

And, as the Viscount had said, he encouraged all those with whom he associated to build up their stables and, more regrettably, to bet on them as he himself had always done.

When everybody had sat down for the second time his neighbour said to the Viscount:

"That was a damned good speech, William. I wish I could make one as easily as you do!"

"It is practice, my dear boy," the Viscount replied. "Like everything else in life, expertise comes with doing the same thing over and over again until one achieves perfection."

"That also applies to love, I suppose?" his friend laughed.

"As you say, in that field as in all others practice makes perfect!"

There was laughter from several other diners who had been listening.

In fact everybody at the table was finding it easy to laugh after a meal which had reached the heights of culinary art and wines that were superlative.

It was always the same at Carlton House, the Viscount told himself. One came away feeling that the King managed to excel at everything he undertook except in gaining the confidence of the people and the popularity he desired.

At dinner-parties like this when he was surrounded by his friends it was impossible not to admire his wit and be almost mesmerised by his charm.

If in nothing else, the King had insisted to those who followed his lead that courtesy and charm were essential to a gentleman.

Morals might have deteriorated during his supremacy in the *Beau Monde*, but good manners had improved out of all recognition just as cleanliness had.

The port was passed round the table and the King

leaned back in his chair, being so witty and so amusing that everybody wished to listen to him rather than to talk among themselves.

However, the evening ended early.

Since he had grown older King George disliked late nights and he had also given up drinking as deeply as he had done when he was young.

Those had known him in the old days could tell stories of how a dinner-party would go on until four o'clock in the morning, when most of the guests left in such a state of inebriation that they had to be carried to their carriages.

But the succession of ladies with whom the King fell in love, starting with Mrs. Fitzherbert, had gradually persuaded him that such roistering was bad for his health.

Now when he rose to his feet in the Royal manner to indicate that it was time to say good-night, a great number of his guests were considering where they should go next.

"Have you an engagement, William? Or shall we go to White's together?" Captain Lionel Worfield asked.

The Viscount considered for a moment.

He was thinking of a very attractive lady who was waiting for him in her *boudoir* in Berkeley Square, and also that at this hour his mistress who was performing at Covent Garden would be hoping that his carriage would be at the Stage Door.

"Is it anything important," he enquired, "or can it wait until tomorrow?"

"It is not exactly urgent," his cousin replied. "But I have had a rather strange letter from Uncle Roderick."

The Viscount stopped.

"You have had a letter?" he enquired and there was no mistaking the surprise in his voice.

"That is what I am telling you," Lionel answered. "Have you had one too?"

"I have!"

Lionel laughed.

"I imagined that you would have. What do you think it means?"

"What it says, I suppose," the Viscount replied.

His carriage came to the door at that moment and without discussing it further both men got into it.

"White's!" the Viscount said to the footman.

As the horses moved off he lay back against the comfortably padded seat and remarked:

"I have often wondered what our estimable uncle intended to do with his millions."

"Is he really as rich as he is reputed to be?" Lionel asked.

"So I understand," the Viscount replied. "Even the Chancellor of the Exchequer speaks of him with a note of awe in his voice!"

"Then what is this girl like when he says he looks on her as his daughter?"

"I have not the slightest idea," the Viscount answered, "but I knew that she had been left his Ward by her father and mother when they died and that he has been introducing her to Social Life in Rome."

"And in Paris," Lionel added. "A friend of mine who was there three months ago described a party Uncle Roderick gave as the most luxurious affair he had ever attended."

The Viscount raised his eye-brows, then said:

"I presume your letter says the same as mine?"

"I have it with me," Lionel answered. "I thought there might be a chance of discussing it with you."

He drew the letter as he spoke, from the inside pocket of his close-fitting coat and handed it to the Viscount.

"I will wait until we are inside the Club," his cousin said. "It is too dark in here to read anything but the greedy expression on your face!"

He laughed as he spoke, taking any sting from his words.

"I admit I could do with a few thousands at the moment, or even hundreds," Lionel replied, "but I am also well aware that with you in the running I have not a chance of being first past the winning-post!"

The Viscount did not contradict him or, if he intended to do so it was too late, because at that moment, Carlton House being only a short distance from White's Club, the horses came to a standstill.

The two cousins walked up the steps and into the most exclusive and important Club in the whole of St. James's, which as usual was packed with their friends.

They extricated themselves with some difficulty from those who wanted to congratulate the Viscount on his win and found a quiet corner in the Coffee Room.

Having ordered drinks from an attentive waiter the Viscount drew out the letter which his cousin had handed him.

He read it slowly:

"My dear Nephew:

I have returned to England after an absence of two years and am re-opening Worfield House where I intend to entertain for my Ward, Astara Beverley.

She is in fact, to all intents and purposes, my daughter, and as I am getting on in years it is her future which concerns me.

The greatest wish of my life is that Astara should marry happily and if possible a member of my family, and live at Worfield House.

It would, I realise, be impossible for any young man to afford the upkeep of such an enormous mansion and the Estate unless I provide for it in my will.

I have therefore decided that my fortune, which as you may be aware is a very considerable one, will be settled jointly on Astara and the man she marries.

It is with this thought in mind that I invite you to come to Worfield House at the earliest possible opportunity to make Astara's acquaintance.

It will also give me great pleasure to see you again and hear of your exploits in the last two years.

With my regards to your parents, I remain your affectionate uncle,

Roderick Worfield."

The Viscount read every word, then returning the letter to his cousin remarked:

"It is identical to the one I received, and written in the same hand."

"You mean that Uncle Roderick did not write it himself?"

"No, of course he did not. And I do not mind betting you, Lionel, that it was inscribed by Astara Beverley."

Lionel Worfield regarded the letter with interest.

"Now that you mention it," he said, "the writing is distinctive – yes, by Gad – it is feminine!"

"I presume our uncle and Astara have between them concocted this idea of having us on show," the Viscount said.

"Well, as I have already told you," Lionel remarked, "it is just a waste of time my journeying to Hertfordshire if you intend to go there."

"None but the brave . . .!" the Viscount teased.

". . deserve the fair!" Lionel finished. "But how do we know she is fair!"

"She is not only fair, she is extremely beautiful!" the Viscount replied.

"Who told you that?"

"Some friends who met her in Rome. In fact they informed me that she will be the toast of St. James's within a week of appearing in London."

"You are making me curious."

"You should be anyway. Think of the money, Lionel. I cannot believe you find it easy to pay your way in the Regiment. I have always been told that the Life Guards are extremely pricey!"

"They are indeed!" Lionel said ruefully, "and since the Regent keeps on fiddling about with our uniform it has become more expensive still."

"Then you certainly need to be an applicant for the hand of the fair Astara!"

"Do you imagine it is some kind of competition?"

"No, I do not think that exactly," the Viscount

answered, "quite seriously I think we are to be paraded in front of this girl as if we were taking part in a joust like the Knights of old. Then she will bestow her favour, doubtless a scented handkerchief, on the man of her choice."

"My God!" Lionel ejaculated. "You make it sound quite nauseating! I am damned if I want to take part in theatricals of that sort."

"I find it rather amusing," the Viscount said. "I have always liked Uncle Roderick and admired him. My father says that he is the genius of the family and certainly that is true where money is concerned."

"Are you hard up?" Lionel asked bluntly.

"Of course I am!" the Viscount replied. "Are we not all in the same boat?"

"Topsail won you 500 guineas to-day."

"That will keep my stable going for about a month."

"Well, I do not suppose there is a man in this Club who does not owe money to the Usurers, not to mention his tailor."

"All the more reason why we should play games with Uncle Roderick," the Viscount retorted. "Do not be a bore, join in the fun!"

"If you are quite certain it will be fun," his cousin replied. "But I have no wish to leave London at the moment. I have just met the most delectable creature, and if I am away for long someone might snatch her from me."

"If you mean that red-haired charmer I saw you with last night I might even do so myself!" the Viscount laughed.

"You dare!" his cousin remarked. "If you lay hands on Clarise, or even so much as smile at her in that manner which draws women into your arms as if you were a magnet, I swear I . . .'

He stopped suddenly.

"Were you intending to call me out?" the Viscount enquired.

"I would certainly want to do so if you interfered

between me and Clarise," his cousin said honestly. "But quite frankly, I have no intention of spending the next two months with my arm in a sling."

The Viscount laughed.

"You are very complimentary, Lionel."

"Unfortunately, I am only speaking the truth."

"Clarise or no Clarise, you would do better to come with me to Worfield House."

"When?"

"To-morrow. The sooner the better. We may have more competitors!"

"There are no other Worfields, as far as I can remember."

"Except for Vulcan," the Viscount said casually.

"Vulcan? Oh, yes, of course. The parson's son! I do not think I fear any competition from him!"

'No, nor do I," the Viscount agreed. "I am, in fact, almost certain he will not be there even if he had been asked. The last time I heard of him – oh, several years ago – he was trekking across the Sahara, or some such outlandish place."

"My father was saying only the other day," Lionel remarked, "what an amazingly successful family we are, with of course one exception."

The Viscount laughed.

"One of my earliest memories of my father and my grandfather is of both of them being in a seething rage because Uncle Luke had turned down the Deanery of Westminster."

"I never saw much of him," Lionel said, "but he always seemed an awfully kind person. I remember he came to my Confirmation when nobody else would take the trouble. He took me out to luncheon and although he was an ordinary village Parson he was so distinguished-looking that one of the boys asked if he was the Archbishop of Canterbury!"

The Viscount laughed.

"The family good looks! Your father was right, Lionel,

we are not only outstandingly clever, but also outstandingly handsome!"

"You are!" Lionel said. "That is why all those delectable creatures whom I entertain from Covent Garden and Drury Lane gravitate towards you like flies towards a honey-pot!"

"I am not certain that is a simile I particularly care for!" the Viscount replied.

At the same time he smiled good-humouredly.

His cousin might be an excellent soldier, but there was no doubt that when it came to a turn of phrase he was far behind the family in that accomplishment.

The Viscount drew his watch from his waist-coat pocket.

It was a very expensive gold watch which had been given to him by a lady who had loved him desperately.

"Whenever you look at the time, dearest William," she had said, "I want you to think of me, because I shall be thinking of you every hour, every minute, every second until we are together again."

The watch, however, at the moment reminded the Viscount not of its giver, but of the eager lips and the soft arms that were waiting for him in Berkeley Square.

He finished the glass in front of him and said to his cousin:

"I will pick you up at about three o'clock to-morrow afternoon with my new team which cost me a monkey. It will not take us more than an hour-and-a-half to reach Worfield House. Our servants can go ahead in the Landau and warn Uncle Roderick of our arrival."

"How long will we be expected to stay?" Lionel asked.

"I think that will depend upon Astara," the Viscount replied.

He rose to start moving with some difficulty through the crowd of his friends towards the front door.

. . . .

Sir Roderick learnt of his two nephews' arrival with a smile of satisfaction.

"I told you they would not be long in obeying your summons," he said to Astara.

"I have asked the Housekeeper to prepare three Bed-Rooms," she answered. "I suppose your nephew Vulcan will stay with us even though he lives so near?"

"It is not as near as you think," Sir Roderick replied.

Astara looked puzzled.

"When I gave the letter to the Butler and asked him to have it delivered, he said it would take the groom less than half-an-hour."

Sir Roderick smiled.

"That is true because the groom would go to Little Milden through the wood by a twisting path which is suitable only for a horse or for someone on foot."

"And by road?" Astara enquired.

"Little Milden is about four miles away."

"How extraordinary!"

"Not really," Sir Roderick replied. "My father, like my grandfather, refused categorically to have any roads built on the Estate. There we have only the main drive and cart-tracks, which is rather surprising when you think we extend over three thousand acres and are still within easy reach of London."

"I think your father was right," Astara said. "It is so lovely to feel that the outside world does not encroach, and as you said to me yesterday Worfield Estate is self-sufficient, almost a State in itself!"

She had in fact been extremely impressed by everything Sir Roderick had shown her.

There had not only been the farms, the granaries, the mills which were all operated by his own employees, but there were also carpenters, stone-masons, smiths, and the foresters besides the enormous amount of offices appertaining to the house itself.

In their travels Astara had visited Palaces of many minor Royalties, and in France had stayed in ancient Châteaux which had not been destroyed or devastated by the Revolution.

But nothing had prepared her for the magnificence of a great ancestral house in England which in a country untouched by war carried on the life and traditions that had been laid down for generations earlier.

"I want you to understand the workings of the Estate," Sir Roderick had said to Astara, "because one day all this will be yours."

She looked at him in a startled fashion.

"Are you not being a little over-optimistic?" she asked. "And you gave me your . . promise that you would not . . make me marry anybody I did not . . wish to."

"I am trusting my luck and my judgement," Sir Roderick said, "and it has stood me in good stead in the past."

He looked at Astara, then laughed softly.

"Why are you laughing?" she asked.

"Because," he answered, "up to now I have always dealt with men and money and found them quite predictable. But now I am dealing with a woman which is new and hitherto unexplored ground."

"That is untrue, and you are an old humbug!" Astara retorted. "You know you are and were a great success with many lovely ladies. An old flirt of yours in Rome told me that she had loved you to distraction but realised she was only one of many!"

"Like all women she was exaggerating!" Sir Roderick said. "But you only confirm my confidence that, if I am as experienced as you are trying to make out, I shall not now make a fundamental mistake."

"That of course remains to be seen," Astara said provocatively.

When she was choosing her gown the following morning, having in mind that Sir Roderick's nephews would be arriving, she wondered with a cynicism that was unnatural to her, if it really mattered what she wore.

Then she told herself that was an unfair view of the two men whom Sir Roderick had described to her so vividly.

Would the Viscount, with all his attainments, or Lionel

Worfield, be willing to give up their freedom just for the sake of money?

Surely they would want to be in love with any woman they made their wife, just as she wanted to be in love with the man who was to become her husband?

After luncheon when she came downstairs carrying her bonnet and a sunshade and had reached the Hall the Butler asked:

"Could you tell me, Miss, if you will be four for dinner or five, as you suggested yesterday?"

"I really do not know, Hedges," Astara answered. "Was there a reply to the letter you arranged to be carried to the Old Mill at Little Milden?"

"The groom informed me, Miss, that although he knocked on the door for some time there was no answer."

"He brought the letter back?" Astara enquired.

"Oh, no, Miss. He slipped it under the door."

"Perhaps Mr. Vulcan Worfield is away."

"No, Miss. The groom was intelligent enough to make some enquiries in the village and he was told that Mr. Worfield was at home, but often, if his servants are out and he's busy, no-one answers the door."

"Busy?" Astara questioned.

The Butler obviously had no more to say on the matter and she proceeded to the Library where Sir Roderick was waiting for her.

"We have received no answer from your nephew Vulcan Worfield," she said.

"That does not surprise me," Sir Roderick answered. "Doubtless he will turn up when it suits him, like a bad penny!"

"I have a feeling you are rather harsh on him," Astara teased. "I only hope that Viscount Yelverton will live up to his reputation."

"I am quite sure he will!" Sir Roderick replied. "In fact Barnes was telling me a little while ago that the whole village backed his horse, Topsail, out of loyalty to the family and are all delighted at what was undoubtedly a sensational win."

Astara had already read the description of the race in the morning newspaper and she knew that it had pleased her uncle.

"Horses are certainly one thing you and William will have in common," he said now. "I was thinking last night that you ride exceptionally well and when I provide you with even better horses than are here already you will be unrivalled."

"I have a feeling I am being groomed to add glamour and sparkle to the Worfield image," Astara laughed. "It will be a terrible thing if by some miscalculation on your part I am a flop and a failure like poor Vulcan."

"You could never be that," Sir Roderick said positively.

He looked critically at Astara for the moment. Then he said:

"Every day you grow more like your mother, and therefore every day in my eyes more beautiful and more alluring. As you suggested yourself, I only wish I were forty years younger! I promise you I should be a most ardent wooer!"

Astara laughed, but her eyes were tender because she knew that Sir Roderick was speaking from his heart.

She was well aware that he was spoken of as a hard and ruthless man by those who did business with him.

She also knew that he could be very critical and cutting if things did not please him.

But he had never shown her anything but tenderness, and she loved the quickness of his mind and the way he never commanded her to do anything but made every effort to understand her point of view.

"You are a very wonderful person, Uncle Roderick," she said now and kissed his cheek.

"Come along. We have a lot to do this afternoon before my nephews' arrival," he said. "I want your advice on what improvements I can make to the garden and to-morrow I have an expert from Kew coming to advise us on the hot-houses."

"That is something in which I am really interested," Astara said. "Flowers make such a difference in every woman's life and in every home."

"That is because women are like flowers themselves," Sir Roderick replied, "or it is what they should be."

He thought, although he did not say so, that Astara was like some unique flower to be found only in far-off places, for which men who were interested in horticulture would risk their lives.

Then with a quick turn of his mind he ceased thinking for the moment of Astara but of the improvements he intended to make not only in the garden, but also in the house and over the whole Estate.

They spent such an absorbing afternoon that when they returned to the house Astara had only just tidied herself and descended to the Salon for tea when the Viscount and Captain Lionel Worfield arrived.

She heard their voices in the Hall as they greeted their uncle, then the door of the Salon opened and he came in followed by, Astara had to admit at first glance, two of the most handsome men she had ever seen.

"Astara, our guests have arrived," Sir Roderick said. "I want you first to meet William who, as I have told you, is my oldest nephew."

As Astara curtsied the Viscount bowed with grace that belied his athletic build and broad shoulders.

She thought that his grey eyes held as questioning an expression as her own.

It was almost, she thought, as if they were puppets being manipulated by Sir Roderick, and she wondered if the Viscount resented the fact.

There was something so theatrical about the whole idea, and the letter which she had written at Sir Roderick's instigation, that she had begun to find it all rather amusing.

It was only when she thought of the future and that she

might really have to choose a husband from among three unknown young men that she felt a little tremor of fear.

But now she told herself such feelings were quite unnecessary and she was certain that the Viscount would prove to be as attractive as he was good-looking.

It was almost startling to realise that Captain Lionel Worfield, when his uncle introduced him, was in his own way as outstandingly handsome as his cousin.

While the Viscount was fair, Lionel's hair was brown and he wore a small military moustache. He had a slim waist which Astara was aware would make him look outstanding in uniform and on a horse.

She busied herself with pouring out the tea and as the gentlemen accepted the cups she handed them, she thought it was only an act of politeness and they would have preferred a glass of wine.

Astara was experienced enough after her time abroad to know that it was Lionel Worfield who looked at her first with an unmistakable admiration in his eyes.

There was also a note in his voice when he addressed her which she recognised.

She had made a conquest and there could be no doubt about that. But she sensed that the Viscount was either more reserved or unwilling to make up his mind too quickly.

Then she thought to herself, perhaps he might be blasé because he was obviously acclaimed and sought after by almost every woman he met.

Sir Roderick made things very easy by talking of old times, enquiring after his brothers, and telling his nephews of the improvements he had decided to make on the Estate.

"Astara is delighted with Worfield House," he said almost boastfully. "As for the garden I had almost forgotten myself how beautiful it can be in the spring."

"It is nice to think that you are in residence again, Uncle Roderick," Lionel remarked.

Sir Roderick rose to show him a picture of his father

when he was a young man, and Astara and the Viscount were left alone at the tea-table.

"Is this your first visit to England, Miss Beverley?" he enquired.

She shook her head.

"No, I lived here on and off until I was twelve," she answered, "and it is very exciting to be back."

"Shall I say how glad I am that you have returned?" the Viscount enquired.

"Only if you mean it," she replied.

"I make up my mind quickly, so may I say in all sincerity that I do mean it."

"Thank you," she smiled.

He noticed that she was not confused or in the least overwhelmed by what he had said.

He had somehow expected because she was so young that she would be, like most of the young girls whom he had met, tongue-tied and stammering and blushing when he spoke to them.

Looking at her a little more closely he realised that she had a polish and a sophistication which he usually connected with much older women.

He felt suddenly as if any reservations that had been in his mind slipped away.

He had expected from what he had already learnt that his uncle's protégée would be attractive, but he saw that Astara had a beauty that was different, although he was not certain how, from any woman he had ever seen.

"If you are finding everything here new and interesting," he said, "I feel much the same. I have not stayed in this house since I was very young. In his old age, our grandfather found us rather bores, and when Uncle Roderick inherited he was so often away that when he did come home he preferred to entertain his contemporaries."

"Nevertheless, he has kept informed of all you have done and your many achievements," Astara replied.

"I am quite certain that is in great part due to my

mother, who is an inveterate letter-writer," the Viscount said.

"I think even if she were not that Uncle Roderick would always find out what he wanted to know about anyone. I sometimes accuse him of compiling a whole encyclopaedia of information on people who interest him."

The Viscount looked startled.

"Does that make you feel apprehensive?" Astara asked.

"No, but it surprises me," he answered. "I thought Uncle Roderick was too busy for family matters."

"On the contrary, I assure you his family is very important to him."

"Then I am very glad to hear it."

There was a note of complacent satisfaction in his voice and Astara remembered that he was the oldest nephew and she thought that the same idea had come to the Viscount's mind.

It would be traditional for Sir Roderick to pass his fortune on to his nephew William, and to ensure that he lived at Worfield House.

She had already learnt that William's father, the Earl of Yelverton, through his wife had acquired an estate in Kent.

William would come into that one day, but she was certain that it was nothing like as magnificent as Worfield.

She had in fact only in the last two days understood why Sir Roderick had said it would be impossible without a huge fortune to keep the place going.

It was one of the largest ancestral houses in Great Britain and required an army of servants to keep it clean, besides all the outside departments which had made her call it a State.

Looking at the Viscount from under her eye-lashes she told herself he would certainly look right as the owner of Worfield.

She could imagine him entertaining in the grand

manner of which his uncle would approve, playing his part in County Affairs and doubtless in time representing the King as Lord Lieutenant of Hertfordshire.

It all seemed cut and dried, a story of which one knew the ending from the moment one started to read the first page.

Then she asked herself what did she feel about William as a man? And what did he feel about her?

Supposing they had met each other in different circumstances?

Supposing he was poor and a nobody and she was unimportant – just Miss Beverley without the aura of Sir Roderick's fortune behind her?

She looked up at the Viscount enquiringly and as if he sensed that she was thinking about him, he bent forward to say:

"You are beautiful, far more beautiful than I anticipated or had hoped!"

"You have heard about me?"

"About your success in Rome. I have a friend who met you out there. What he told me was not flattering, I realise that now. Merely factual."

She smiled.

"You are beginning to sound like the Italians who manage to make everything they say sound like a compliment."

"It is not difficult when one is speaking to someone like you."

Astara smiled again but she was quite composed and very sure of herself.

"I think, My Lord," she said after a moment, "as we both have heard so much about each other, that it is important that we should use our own minds to determine what is true and what is not."

"That is what I always do myself," the Viscount said. "I have never yet taken a reference on any servant I have employed, and I seldom bother to look at the pedigree of a horse before I buy it."

"In the East they call that 'using one's third eye'," Astara murmured.

He looked puzzled and she explained:

"There is an old legend that in the distant past the first human being had only one eye in the centre of his forehead. Then he developed two more and the middle eye was lost."

"But you are suggesting that it is still there."

Astara nodded.

"That is the eye we use when we judge people by what they are to us and not just by what we have heard about them."

"Then I hope your third eye will be working where I am concerned," the Viscount said.

"I would say the same to you."

"It is already," the Viscount smiled. "Shall I tell you now what I feel about you? Or would you rather wait until later?"

"I think I would rather wait until you are quite certain," Astara replied. "'He who travels slowly . . arrives safely'."

"As we will!" the Viscount said firmly.

Then Sir Roderick came back to the table and there was no chance of any further intimate conversation.

Astara, however, soon had her chance, or rather was manoeuvred by Sir Roderick into having it, of being alone with Lionel Worfield.

Deliberately, but so cleverly that Astara was amused, Sir Roderick took the Viscount onto the terrace to show him a new strain of deer which had been introduced to the Park.

She had left the tea-table to seat herself on a sofa and Lionel joined her.

"You are very different from what I expected," he said bluntly, and when she looked surprised he added:

"That sounds rude, but I do not mean it to be. It is just because you are English by birth, I did not expect you to look un-English."

"I always thought I looked very English with my fair hair and blue eyes," Astara protested.

"They are certainly traditional," Lionel agreed, "but while they are beautiful there is something unusual in your appearance which I did not expect."

"I think perhaps it is because my great-grandmother was Greek and therefore I am not entirely English," Astara explained.

"Then that was perceptive of me, was it not?" Lionel exclaimed. "Did William say the same thing?"

"No. Why should you think he would?"

"Only that we were discussing what you would be like on our way down here. My father has often told me how fond he was of your father, and William said the same. I suppose we both expected a beautiful young Englishwoman out of the same mould."

Astara laughed.

"You are certainly frank, Captain Worfield."

"Do you not think that as we share Uncle Roderick, we might use each other's Christian names?" he asked. "I will call you Cousin Astara, if you like, but it is rather a mouthful."

"Are you being complimentary in accepting me so quickly as a relative?" Astara asked.

"You are so much more attractive and certainly a thousand times lovelier than any of my other relatives," Lionel replied, "that I am only too willing to accept you in any capacity. But I know which one I prefer."

He was starting to woo her very quickly, and she had the feeling that he was making the most of having her to himself while William was out on the terrace with Sir Roderick.

"Thank you," she said aloud, "and I shall be delighted if I may call you Lionel and if you would call me Astara."

"You must meet my father," Lionel said. "He is a great authority on Greece. I believe he once spent a whole of one vacation there when he was up at Oxford. Anyway,

Greek Literature is what he reads for relaxation, although I cannot say it appeals to me."

"What do you read?" Astara enquired.

"Very little," he confessed honestly, "except the newspapers and that sort of thing. To tell you the truth, and you might as well know the worst at once, I am not really clever like the rest of my family."

"But I am told you are very brave," she said softly.

"I try to be a good soldier," he answered, "and if I am honest I rather enjoy a battle."

Astara did not answer and after a moment he went on:

"Perhaps a woman would not understand this, but there is something very exhilarating in challenging an enemy, in matching oneself and one's men against his."

"You are also risking your life."

"One does not think about that at the time. Afterwards, if one is still alive, one thanks God for the fact, but when actually fighting a soldier is concerned only with being the victor."

She saw by the light in his eyes and by hearing the enthusiasm in his voice that he was right when he said it was an exhilarating experience.

She liked the way he was honest about himself and his interests. She liked too the way he looked at her because there was something open and almost boyish about it.

"I must say you are a surprise," he said. "I very nearly did not come here, but I am extremely glad now that I did."

"You would have refused your uncle's invitation?"

"I thought there was not much point in my answering it as William was coming too."

Astara looked at him with a smile on her lips as he explained:

"You see, William is such a hell of a chap, a Corinthian and all that sort of thing, that I do not get much of a chance to shine."

"I have a feeling you do so in battle," Astara said.

"I enjoy myself in the Regiment, but when it comes to social success, well – William is always there first."

"I think you are being ultra-modest. Uncle Roderick said some very nice things about you, and if you take my advice you will be yourself and not worry about your cousin."

"Do you mean that?"

There was an eagerness in Lionel's voice which told her she had said more than she intended.

She had not in fact been thinking of him as a suitor, but merely as a rather engaging young man who had an inferiority complex where his cousin was concerned.

Now she thought almost in dismay that she had perhaps encouraged him too obviously.

"I may be mistaken," she said quickly, "but perhaps it would be wise if we made no decisions about each other or about William until we know each other better."

"I feel I know you already," Lionel said, "and I am quite certain of one thing."

"What is that?" Astara asked.

"That I am going to make the very best of my chances before William and every daring young Buck in London snatches you away from under my very nose!"

Astara laughed, for she could not help it.

Then as Sir Roderick and William came back into the Salon from the terrace she saw the expression on the Viscount's face and realised that he was annoyed.

CHAPTER THREE

Astara entered the shadows of the trees and started to walk along the mossy path which led through the wood towards Little Milden.

She had just seen Sir Roderick, William and Lionel off from the front door.

They had decided to visit the Horse Fair in Potters Bar which took place twice a year. The Viscount had told his uncle there were sometimes decent horses to be found there, especially foals.

"A friend of mine purchased a horse there four years ago which has now won him five races," he said. "It is not in the top class, but undoubtedly it was an outstanding bargain."

Sir Roderick's interest was aroused and so was Lionel's.

"Let us go and have a look at what we can find," he said quickly. "There are several chaps in my Regiment in need of cheap horses at the moment. If I can provide what they want, I might make a little on each purchase."

His uncle smiled.

"That is the right idea, my boy! Always turn an honest penny when you can."

"I am actually looking for some mares," the Viscount said in a lofty manner as if the idea of making a profit on a horse had never entered his mind.

"It will be amusing even if we find nothing which is

good enough for us," Sir Roderick said.

He smiled at Astara as he asked:

"Will you excuse us for one afternoon, my dear? I do not think a Horse Fair is the right place for you."

"Certainly not!" the Viscount agreed positively before Astara could speak. "It can be very rough and there are often fights among the Gypsies."

Astara thought a little wistfully that she might find it interesting.

But as it was quite obvious that the gentlemen did not want her she acquiesced gracefully and after they had finished luncheon waved them good-bye from the steps of the house.

She had, however, had an idea of how she might spend the afternoon and now was the moment to put it into operation.

She was well aware that in the last three days they had been staying at Worfield House both the Viscount and his cousin Lionel were wooing her arduously.

They were very circumspect, especially when they were present together, trying to appear as if they were not concerned with stealing a march on each other.

But whenever it was possible they paid her effusive compliments and made their intentions very clear.

She felt, however, that William was quite confident that she would accept his invitation to be his wife, and that when the time came he would take Sir Roderick's place as owner of the house and the Estate.

Occasionally she even detected him slipping up in something he said and forgetting to disguise his eagerness to be the possessor not only of herself but of his uncle's wealth.

"I shall change that," he had said last night in an unguarded moment.

It had been when they were talking of a feast that was given every Michaelmas to the farmers.

There was a little pause after he had spoken and he added:

"I think it is a custom which is kept over a great deal of the country and is in fact a waste of time and money. The labourers, I am convinced, in most cases would rather have the money in their pocket."

Sir Roderick started to argue with him that the feast and the festivities broke the monotony of a working man's life, especially when he lived in the country, and Astara wondered later whether her uncle had realised exactly what William had implied.

She felt, however, that both Sir Roderick and William himself were pushing her towards a decision and she had not yet made up her own mind which of the two applicants for her hand she really preferred.

There was no doubt that the Viscount was magnificent and she could understand that his sportsmanship and the fact that he was a Corinthian, a leader of the "Four-in-Hand" Club, and an outstanding amateur pugilist appealed to her uncle.

He was certainly handsome to look at and she was sure that under his tight-fitting, well-tailored coat he had rippling muscles which her father had always told her were a tailor's nightmare.

Yet when they all rode together in the mornings she thought that perhaps Lionel was the better rider of the two.

He looked as if he were part of his horse and she had the impression that animals responded to him with affection while they merely obeyed William.

But she was not completely certain of anything about the two cousins.

One moment she found herself favouring William, the next Lionel, and she knew that because they were both on their best behaviour, because they were wooing her, and because she was seeing them always to their advantage, it was very difficult to assess them accurately.

Now as she walked in the shadow of the trees she asked herself frankly whether she really wished to spend the rest of her life with either of them.

What did they have in common with her?

She found that for instance neither of them was particularly interested in books.

This was something that she told herself she had no right to expect; for Sir Roderick was not a great reader except where the Financial columns of the newspapers were concerned.

He could also become immersed in documents which arrived daily from his office in London and which she told herself were as difficult to understand as a foreign language for a person who was not knowledgeable in monetary matters.

But because she loved books, because they meant so much in her life, she wondered if she would find conversation entirely on day to day subjects, which of course would include the local gossip, somewhat restricting.

She realised that William moved in far more important and naturally more scandal-loving society than did Lionel.

The latter was deeply connected with the affairs of his Regiment, and Astara found it interesting to talk to him about Regimental life and the soldiers he commanded.

She was quite certain that if he remained as he obviously wished to do in the Life Guards he would eventually end up as a General, and she questioned whether from her own point of view that was what she would enjoy.

One thing puzzled her and that was why Vulcan Worfield had not replied to his uncle's letter.

She had the feeling that because he had ignored it Sir Roderick had completely dismissed him from his mind and no longer considered him to be an applicant for the "Golden Apple".

"Has there been no message from your third nephew?" she had asked Sir Roderick last night before dinner when she was alone with him.

Sir Roderick shook his head.

"I imagine he has gone abroad again, or else he is just not interested in seeing me," he replied.

She heard the sharpness in his voice.

"Perhaps he did not receive the letter."

"I questioned the groom who took it," Sir Roderick retorted. "He told me he put it through the door and there was therefore no possibility of it being lost in the post or mislaid in any way."

He looked at Astara and added:

"I think we can write Vulcan off as a non-starter."

Astara, however, was looking up at the picture she so admired.

"There were three goddesses," she said. "Hera, Athene and Aphrodite. It does not seem fair somehow that we should forget Vulcan."

"He obviously wishes to be forgotten," Sir Roderick replied.

There was no mistaking now from the tone of his voice that he was annoyed.

Astara was not able to reply as at that moment William and Lionel had come into the Salon.

She found the meals they had together were very amusing.

Each young man vied with the other to be charming and witty and she had always enjoyed Sir Roderick's dry humour.

She knew he was watching her, wondering all the time which she favoured, and there was no doubt if the choice were his who would be the winner.

The weather was warm for April, and walking through the wood Astara slipped off the light shawl she had worn over her gown.

She had deliberately put on a very simple one that she had bought in Italy.

It was deceptively simple because it had been in fact exceedingly expensive and so had the chip-straw bonnet ornamented only with a wreath of wild flowers.

The path twisted and turned through the trees and after a while Astara found her shawl heavy on her arm.

After a moment's thought she laid it down among the

celandines that were in bloom beneath the trees and thought that no-one would notice it if they were passing casually by.

Then as she walked back to the path she took off her bonnet and carried it by its ribbons.

Now she could feel what breeze there was on her hair and the warmth of the sun as it percolated through the boughs above her.

There was the scent of spring in the air and she wanted to stop and pick some of the yellow primroses that grew in profusion in clumps beneath the trees, vying in colour with the wild daffodils.

Then she told herself she had no time and a few minutes later she had her first sight of the thatched roofs of the cottages of Little Milden.

At the edge of the wood she stopped and saw in the distance the square grey tower of a Church.

She had expected also to see a Mill towering above the other roofs, but there was none in sight and she wondered as she came from the wood whether she should turn right or left.

Outside the first cottage she came to was a woman tending to a small boy who had fallen down and grazed his knee.

Astara stopped at the gate.

"Excuse me," she said. "Can you tell me the way to the old Mill?"

The woman glanced up at the sound of her voice and saw that she was bare-headed. She obviously did not think she was Quality and therefore not entitled to a curtsey.

"Ye takes th' left fork where th' road turns," she answered with her soft Hertfordshire accent. "Be ye a-goin' to Mister Worfield?"

"Yes, that is right," Astara answered.

"Then ye tell 'im our Moll'll not be a-comin' to him no more," the woman said.

She spoke sharply. Then as Astara did not reply, she added:

"Ye can tell 'im, if he be interested, that our Moll's took off with a traveller, an' very upset Farmer Jarvis be about it."

"Why should he be that?" Astara asked interestedly.

She was wondering how Moll, whoever she might be, concerned Vulcan Worfield.

"What wi' th' lambing an' th' calving, they be busy up at th' farm at this time o' th' year," the woman explained. "An' Farmer Jarvis thinks it be too bad o' our Moll t' go off wi'out a word. But there, that's girls for ye!"

"Is Moll your daughter?" Astara enquired.

"Aye, me first, an' pretty enough, Oi grant ye that, but wi' never a thought for no-one but 'erself. What Oi says is that Mister Vulcan just panders to 'er conceit. Ever so proud, 'er be if 'e wants 'er up at th' Mill. But that don't help Farmer Jarvis, as Oi tells 'er."

Astara was slightly bewildered, but she thought it would seem inquisitive to ask too many questions.

"You say I take the turn on the left?" she said. "And thank you for helping me."

"That's orl right," the woman said still busy bandaging the small boy's knee. "Don't ee forget t' tell Mister Vulcan that Moll'll be a-coming no more."

"No, I will not forget," Astara promised and walked on.

She found herself extremely curious as to why Vulcan Worfield should want Moll to come to the Mill.

What use could he make of a pretty girl who worked on a farm?

Astara did not like to give an answer to that question. Then as she took the turn to the left she saw ahead of her the old Mill standing by itself at the side of a large pool.

It was not as high a building as she had expected and the great iron wheel which the water had once turned was still and rusty.

The rest of the mill had been painted white and its beams blackened.

It had a picturesque attraction especially as she drew nearer and saw that there was water on both sides of it.

She drew nearer still and saw that the door, and there was only one, was open, and she wondered if it had been left in such a manner because Moll was expected.

She looked for a knocker, but found none, and after hesitating for a moment she walked into the narrow passage in which the walls were painted white and the floor covered rather attractively with old flagstones.

Everything was very quiet and there was only the soft sound of her feet as she moved along feeling that she was on the threshold of an adventure!

At the same time she thought her curiosity and unconventional manner of entering the Mill might be misunderstood.

On the left-hand side of the passageway she saw another door and this too was open and she realised she had found what she sought.

In front of her was a room that she realised stretched from one side of the Mill to the other. It was quite unlike any room she had ever seen before.

She took a step inside and saw a man seated at an easel in front of a window which stretched from floor to ceiling.

He must have heard her, for without turning his head he said sharply:

"You are late as usual! Do not waste time but get on the throne and for Heaven's sake, hurry up!"

He spoke in a deep voice with a note of urgency which made Astara smile.

She had been in artists' Studios before and now she understood why Vulcan Worfield had required Moll to come to the Mill.

The throne on the inevitable artists' dais was at the side of the window. It was draped with a piece of green brocade and lying on a chair was a sheaf of wheat.

"Hurry!" Vulcan Worfield said as Astara stood indecisive, "and try to hold the wheat correctly as a symbol of fertility not as if it was a bundle of old faggots!"

Astara walked across the room and putting her bonnet down on the chair stepped onto the dais.

She picked up the wheat and held it in her arms rather, she thought, in the manner that a woman would hold a child.

She stood quite still and looked at the man who was intent on the canvas which stood on the easel.

"The light was perfect half-an-hour ago!" he grumbled, "but I suppose the farmer kept you and what I am doing is not as important as milking one of those noisy cows."

There was a hint of amusement in his voice now. Then he said in a very different tone:

"If I cannot get your head right to-day, I think I shall go mad!"

He looked up as he spoke and was frozen into immobility.

Now Astara could see his face full on and she realised that Vulcan Worfield was in fact as handsome as his two cousins, but in a very different manner.

Not only was his hair dark, but his skin, doubtless from long exposure to the elements was the warm, golden-brown that she connected with men who came from the East.

He was thin and his cheek-bones were prominent like the sharp lines of his chin. His eyes, surprised by her appearance, were enquiring and at the same time penetrating.

He looked at her for a long moment. She did not move or speak but merely stood in her white gown holding the sheaf of wheat as he had requested her to do.

Then without saying anything Vulcan returned to his picture.

He rubbed out what he had painted and started to use his brush swiftly and decisively.

He worked for several minutes before he asked:

"What is your name?"

Then before Astara could answer he added:

"No, do not tell me! You are Aphrodite and you have come down from Olympus to take the place of a recalcitrant shepherdess!"

Astara did not reply for a moment. Then she said in a low voice:

"Moll could not come."

"Thank God for that!" Vulcan said. "Raise your chin a trifle – that is perfect! Do not move!"

He painted so that his brush seemed to fly over the canvas, looking up at her, then back again while she kept the pose he required.

After what seemed to her to be a long time, he said:

"How could you have known – how could you have been aware that, I needed you so desperately? But then, of course, the cries of mankind have always been heard by the gods when they trouble to listen to them."

"Moll has gone away with a traveller."

"I thought she would succumb to his blandishments in the end," Vulcan remarked. "And why not? He can doubtless give her a fuller life than she would find here."

"Will he marry her?"

Still painting she thought that Vulcan metaphorically shrugged his shoulders.

"I hope not! Cluttered with children she might as well have stayed at home."

"I imagine from the way you speak," Astara said, "that you do not think marriage is a particularly enviable state."

"It is certainly confining both for a man and a woman."

"Then what is the alternative?"

"To be free to roam the world and develop the mind, but perhaps you would not understand that."

"You think I would prefer to be confined with children and, of course, a regular wage coming in every week?"

He glanced up at her to say sharply:

"Keep your chin up! Look up as Persephone would have done towards the sky!"

"Seeking the light?" Astara asked quietly.

"But of course! As if the Greeks ever did anything else!"

He was silent for a moment, then as if he spoke to himself, he quoted:

"'When Apollo poured across the sky flashing with a million points of light, he healed everything he touched and defied the powers of darkness'."

Astara drew in her breath.

It was what she had felt when she had been in Greece with her father and mother that last year before they met their deaths.

She had known that light that had seemed different from any other anywhere in the world, and though it was difficult to put into words, she had felt as if Apollo was there.

She found him in everything she saw; in the waves of the sea, in the fish churning in the nets, in the gleaming eyes of the Greeks themselves, and even in the bare rocks which rose almost threateningly above the valleys.

A light that seemed to have been crystallised and to be more intense, more pure and more spiritual than any other she had known.

Aloud she asked:

"Why are you painting this picture?"

"It is for a book," Vulcan answered briefly.

"What book? Have you written it yourself?"

"Of course!"

"What is it about?"

"I doubt if you would be interested."

"I am interested."

He looked at her again.

"You are perfect! I am prepared to go down on my knees and make any sacrifice to you, or whoever sent you, because you are what I wanted."

"I am glad I can be so . . useful."

"Useful!" he explained. "It is much more than that! I was in despair of ever getting this picture finished on time. But now you are here and I am not certain how I can express my gratitude."

"In time for what?" Astara asked.

"Publication day."

"I asked you what your book is about."

He smiled and she thought it took the hardness from his face.

It was in fact, she told herself, a hard face, the face of a man who might have fought and struggled against tremendous odds.

Then she reminded herself that according to Sir Roderick, Vulcan had just been a waster, a wanderer over the face of the earth with no set purpose.

It was not surprising that Sir Roderick who always applied himself so diligently, spurred on by his ambition to succeed, should despise someone who appeared to him to be just drifting.

"I would like you to tell me what subject you are writing about," Astara insisted, "especially as you tell me I am so . . useful."

"You are useful, and let me tell you that you are at the moment taking part in the mysteries of Eleusis."

Astara smiled. It was what she had expected.

Her father had told her of the great ceremonies that had taken place at Eleusis near Athens, when people gathered from the ends of the earth to attend the mysteries in the Temple and for some of them to be initiated.

She knew that the worshippers gathered there on the nineteenth day of the month at the Double Gate below the Acropolis, for the fourteen-mile journey along the Sacred Way.

They wore purple robes, carried long sticks of fennel and were crowned with myrtle.

The most important part of the long and exhausting ceremony came when Persephone appeared holding a sheaf of corn as one would hold a child.

The Initiates had been kept in darkness, as it were of the underworld, and had been deafened by the sound of rushing waters, by thunder, by music, and by other alarming devices which would lead them into an emotional state where they would be receptive to the final mystery.

Invisible hands had clutched at them and in horror they had been brought almost to the state of madness.

No-one knew, Astara had been told by her father, how long an Initiate wandered in the darkness, until suddenly he emerged into a light that seemed to be of the gods: there would be candles, the brightness of a shrine and Persephone holding in her arms a sheaf of corn.

She would give an ear of corn to the Initiate and a jug filled with water. Then as she commanded: "Let the rain fall! Let the seed flower!" the priests danced round him, for he himself had become part of spring and light.

As it all flashed through Astara's mind, she now knew how Vulcan was painting her.

Yet she wondered how any living painter could depict those sacred moments that were so mysterious that they were untranslatable into words.

Her silence must have surprised Vulcan for after a moment he asked:

"Are you no longer curious, or are you just tired?"

"A little tired, perhaps," Astara admitted.

"Then you may rest," he said, "but only for a short while. I must go on painting just in case I am not blessed by your appearance another day."

Astara put down the sheaf of wheat on a chair, feeling that in fact it had suddenly become very heavy in her arms.

She had sat for two artists in Rome who had painted her portrait, neither to Roderick's satisfaction, and she knew of old how exhausting it was to keep in one position for very long.

She stepped down from the dais and as she did so she asked:

"May I look at your painting?"

She knew that many artists would refuse, but Vulcan replied indifferently:

"If you wish, but I do not suppose for one moment it is the sort of picture you expect."

He spoke almost contemptuously and she had an idea that he supposed she would appreciate only something very conventional and pink-and-white.

She moved to the easel, and what she saw astonished her.

Persephone was in the foreground, but she realised that Vulcan Worfield had tried to portray the mysticism and symbolism she represented.

He was painting it by a method different from that of any other painter she had ever seen, relying on the strokes of his brush and by light and shade to project into the mind what he tried to convey.

There seemed to be no actual form behind the figure of Persephone, and yet in some strange manner it hinted at what the Initiate had passed through in the darkness.

One could almost hear the crack of the whips, the stones which had fallen on him, the smoke which had choked him, the snakes which had clung to him.

Here was everything that aroused terror and then in the foreground illuminating Persephone was the light of initiation.

The picture was not finished, but even so the whole story was there, and yet Astara wondered if she was seeing with her eyes or only in her mind.

"Well?" Vulcan asked. "Why not say you are disappointed as I know you must be?"

He spoke almost jeeringly, and Astara knew that he did not imagine for one moment that she would have the least conception of what he was trying to convey.

She did not answer, but just stood there, seeing also that he had portrayed her in a manner that made her almost afraid.

It was certainly no conventional portrait and her features were blurred, and yet the eyes were definitely hers.

It was as if he had tried to convey not only the feelings of the Initiate for what he had been through, but also those of Persephone – the joy of coming back to the upper earth, the wonder of being united with the light after the four long months of darkness in Hades.

He had made Persephone very young which was

correct because the ceremony itself had been one of youth.

The young corn, the young goddess, and yet Astara felt there was more than that in this picture. There was something of herself, of her uncertainty and of her fear.

It was only an impression, but it was unmistakable. She tried to think it was what he had intended to portray long before she had come to the old Mill, but she could not help feeling it was something personal.

"Tell me," his voice said beside her. "Tell me what you think."

"It is not a question of thinking," Astara replied, "but of feeling, and that is what I am doing."

She looked up at him as she spoke and he stared at her for several seconds before he asked:

"Why do you say that?"

She smiled.

"I believe you are Aphrodite!" he exclaimed. "You are not real – not human!"

"I am as you have painted me," Astara said, "and it makes me a little afraid."

"I knew you were afraid," he answered, "but not of me?"

She shook her head.

"Of myself."

"As Persephone was until the light reassured her," he said.

"As I would like to be reassured."

She felt as if they were both talking in a dream and she saw the surprise in his dark eyes and knew she was vividly conscious of him as a man.

He was wearing the blue artist's smock favoured by Parisian painters and he was tall and somehow overpowering. But it was not his physical presence, she thought, but rather the vibrations which seemed to emanate from him which affected her.

With an effort, because she was afraid of what she might say if they went on talking, she said:

"I am ready to . . continue if you are."

"No, wait a moment," he replied. "I want to know who you are and why you have come here."

He spoke as if he was forcing himself to think clearly and to come back to earth and commonplace matters.

"Does it matter?" Astara asked. "Moll's mother sent me. Is that not enough?"

"It should be," he replied, "but I am curious."

She moved away as if she was afraid he would force from her what she was not yet ready to tell.

"May I look around your Studio?"

He made a gesture with his hand.

"It is all yours!"

He glanced at his picture and without a word sat down in front of it, as if it drew him and he found it difficult to concentrate on anything else.

Astara walked across the room.

She realised that besides the great north window there was another on the other side looking south.

The curtains had been pulled over it and she saw that the material of which they were made was richly embroidered satin.

She thought they looked Chinese and she saw that the rugs on the floor were Persian and of a very fine quality.

She guessed such things had been acquired by Vulcan on his travels.

But the walls which were painted white were bare with the exception of the place over the mantelpiece where there was hung a Rangda or Witch Mask that she knew came from the East, perhaps from the Bali where they believed the masks would keep away evil.

It was all very fascinating and quite unlike what she would have expected in a Mill which had become the home of a parson's son.

Then she told herself she might have expected that no Worfield would be ordinary nor could there be anything mediocre about them.

She looked at the furniture and saw that some of it was oak.

There was a Jacobean chest exquisitely carved which might have belonged to his parents, a small refectory table and a desk that her uncle would have been proud to own. She suspected it had been made in the reign of James II.

Everything on it was very neatly arranged which surprised her, since she had thought that all artists were untidy. But there was an almost meticulous tidiness about the papers, a few books and in the centre a strangely shaped ink-pot that was obviously of foreign origin.

In front of this she saw, arranged one upon the other, a number of letters. They were unopened and quite clearly she could recognise, half-hidden beneath another envelope, her own writing.

Astara smiled to herself. This was the explanation why Vulcan had not come to Worfield House. He simply had not read the invitation.

Yet it seemed strange that he should not have opened his letters but had arranged them neatly and carefully on his desk.

She wondered how she could broach the subject to him; how she could persuade him at least to be aware that his uncle wished to see him.

Then she told herself perhaps it would be more amusing to leave things as they were, and let him believe she was just a friend of Moll's.

As if he knew what she was thinking he said, without turning round:

"What are you doing in Little Milden? I cannot believe that you are working on a farm."

"I am staying in the . . vicinity."

"Then that is my good fortune."

"I am glad you think so, and may I say I admire your house?"

"What particularly do you admire about it, apart, of course, from my pictures?"

"Your curtains are very beautiful."

"They came from China."

"You have been to China?"

"Yes. Come back. I want to get the light in your eyes right. You need not hold the sheaf."

She obeyed him, stepping back onto the throne and falling naturally into the pose she had assumed before.

"That is it! Perfect! The light has faded, however. For Heaven's sake to-morrow try to come as early as possible. The days are so short."

There was a pause before Astara replied:

"I have not . . said that I can . . come to-morrow."

"But you have to! I want you!"

"I think perhaps this time of day would be . . impossible."

"For goodness sake, girl, have you got yourself tied up in some ridiculous employment? Whatever you are earning I will give you more."

"It is not a question of money."

"Then what?"

Astara thought frantically what she would say.

"I have . . certain important commitments," she answered eventually.

"Commitments? What commitments? Nothing at the moment is more important than that I should get this picture right!"

Astara did not answer for a moment. Then she said:

"Your picture is for the book."

"It will have to be engraved which will not detract in any way from what I am trying to express. It will also be exhibited."

"Where?"

"In Paris."

Astara was surprised.

"In Paris?"

"Does that astonish you? Well, I will explain, although it is doubtful if you will know what I am talking about."

Astara felt angered by his insinuation that she was so stupid but she said nothing and he went on:

"Next year the French are forming a *Société des Géographes* and one of the first books which they have decided to publish will be mine. The pictures I have drawn especially for it will be on show."

Vulcan spoke casually in a manner which told Astara he did not think she would understand for a moment what he was saying, but she did.

Just before they had come to England her uncle had taken her to a dinner-party given by some of the leading intellectuals in Paris, and among them had been a very distinguished man who had known her father.

They had talked of the discoveries that were being made all over the world and he said:

"If only your father were alive, Miss Beverley, I know he would have been interested in learning that next year I am founding a *Société des Géographes* and starting off with an exhibition which will be contributed to by almost all the explorers who are still alive."

"Papa would have been thrilled!" Astara said.

"He would certainly have contributed to my exhibition and I should have asked him to give quite a number of lectures."

The gentleman to whom Astara was speaking had paused before he continued:

"Your father always made everything he described so interesting. If only he had put down on paper a great deal more of his travels than we have in our files."

"Papa always found it a nuisance to have to write down what he felt and thought about the places he visited."

Astara had smiled before she added:

"I think perhaps he was a rather selfish explorer. He did it for his own pleasure and did not worry about posterity."

She thought now that Vulcan Worfield was different. He at least had completed a book and she knew that she was exceedingly curious as to what it contained.

At the same time she did not wish to say too much or make him suspicious as to who she might be.

She did not know why, but she suddenly decided she would keep her identity a complete secret from him.

He had not opened the letter that she had written to him on her uncle's behalf. He obviously had no idea that Sir Roderick was in residence at Worfield House.

Something in the manner in which he was concentrating on his painting told her that he was a man who gave himself whole-heartedly to whatever he was occupied on at the moment.

There was an interruption; someone came into the room and while Astara heard them and was conscious they were there she did not turn her head.

"I am back, Master."

A man spoke in a strange sing-song voice.

"I expect my model would like some tea, Chang."

"Yes, Master. Rose petal, or Jasmine?"

Astara saw the smile on Vulcan's lips as for a moment he looked towards her.

"Which is your choice?" he asked. "Or would you prefer the heavy brew of coarse leaves which the English call tea?"

"I would like Jasmine, please," Astara replied.

"Strange," Vulcan remarked. "I have never before met a woman who did not ask for rose petal."

He looked at his picture and went on:

"But then you are different – very different – and as I have told you already I am curious."

"You have told me too that I am Aphrodite and surely you remember that the gods were always punished for being too inquisitive."

"So you know your mythology!" he said. "I am becoming more and more intrigued, Aphrodite, if that is your name."

"Shall I say I will . . answer to it?"

"What woman could resist being mysterious?" he asked. "However, if you want to play games I am quite prepared to do so as long as you will pose for me, although Heaven knows how I can reward you for doing so."

"What did Moll receive?" Astara asked with a smile.

"Four pence an hour," Vulcan replied. "And may I add she thought it considerably more than she was worth."

"I am afraid I am rather more expensive."

"What do you intend to ask of me? Half of my Kingdom? As you can see, there is not much of it."

"I will think of something," Astara replied, "and may I say that your Kingdom, as you call it, is very attractive. I wondered why it was so tidy. Now I know who was responsible."

"You mean Chang. I cannot imagine what a mess I would be in without him."

"Did you bring him here from China?"

"Yes. He had attached himself to me and chose me as his Master. I really had no say in the matter."

"I believe the Chinese are excellent servants."

Vulcan laughed.

"Chang is much more than that. He is my companion, my friend, and at times regrettably like the old Nanny who fussed over me when I was a child."

"When you lived in the Vicarage?"

"So you know that!" Vulcan exclaimed. "It was an ideal place to live and doubtless formed my character before I was seven which the Jesuits say are the most important years of our lives."

"What was the Vicarage like?" Astara asked.

"It was a large, rambling house," Vulcan replied, "and quite unsuitable for the impoverished stipend of most village parsons. There were ghosts in the corridors and banshees screaming round the chimneys when there was a storm."

He smiled and continued:

"There were huge cellars which I was quite certain highwaymen had used when being pursued and an enormous wild garden in which I believed there were Red Indians and whole gangs of murderous savages!"

Astara laughed.

"You obviously had far too much imagination for one small boy."

"I had to make up for being an only child."

"As I was."

"Then we have one bond in common," Vulcan said, "for 'only' children are usually different from other people."

"In what way?"

"They are closer to the immaterial world. They see and hear with a sharpened perception simply because they have time to develop their senses as other children squabbling and moving about in a crowd are unable to do."

"I never thought of that," Astara said, "but I think it is true."

"That is why my picture made you feel," Vulcan said. "You were not lying? It did make you feel what I was trying to say?"

"It made me . . feel," Astara repeated as if he forced her to do so.

"Tell me what you felt," he insisted.

Almost without choosing her words Astara quoted the rhetorican Aristides, and said very quietly:

"'Of all the divine graces accorded to man Eleusis is the most terrible and the most marvellous!'"

Even as she spoke Vulcan turned to look at her and she saw the astonishment in his eyes.

"Who in the name of God are you?" he asked. "How do you know such things, and how can you have come to me of all people?"

Astara smiled, then fortunately before she had to think of an answer Chang came into the room carrying a tray.

"May I drink my Jasmine tea?" she asked.

"I suppose I shall have to let you," Vulcan replied grudgingly. "And you are making it difficult for me to work."

"I am sorry about that. Shall I keep silent?"

"Even if you do I shall still be thinking of you and wondering what you would say if you spoke."

"It seems I cannot do right. At the same time you must

curb your curiosity, or perhaps I shall leave you and never return."

She spoke on purpose provocatively and Vulcan rose from the stool.

"You dare to do that!" he said. "I swear I will curse you and you may be sure I know some very effective ones!"

"I am not afraid," Astara replied. "You may have the power to curse, but, of course, as Aphrodite I have the antidote."

"Love itself can be a curse."

"Is that what you have . . found?"

"Now who is being curious?" he enquired.

They both moved across the room to where on a small table Chang had laid a cloth and set down the tea-things.

The tea was made in a Chinese pot and the handleless cups were of the most exquisite porcelain.

Astara touched one gently.

"How beautiful!" she exclaimed. "Now I know why you wished to have somewhere to put all these treasures. Will you show me the rest of the old Mill before I leave?"

"When do you have to leave?" Vulcan asked.

Astara thought quickly.

She doubted if her uncle and cousins would be home before five o'clock but she must be there before them.

"And when you leave where are you going?" Vulcan enquired before she spoke. "You cannot imagine that I shall let you just vanish in case, as you threaten, you do not reappear."

Pouring out the tea into the exquisite cups Astara said:

"I promise you I will come again, but it may not be at the exact time you wish me to do so."

"I shall be grateful for small mercies," he said. "They may be very small, but at least you will come."

"I will try. Please believe me that I will try, but I cannot promise what might be impossible."

Vulcan had seated himself at the small table.

Now he rose to pull back the curtains that had covered the south window.

The sunlight flooded in in golden rays touching Astara's bare head and bringing into prominence the red lights in her hair.

He stood looking at her before he seated himself once again beside her at the table.

"Let me look at you," he said. "You are not English?"

"Not entirely. I am partly Greek . . ."

"Greek!" he interrupted. "I could tell it was Greek by the shape of your nose."

". . a little way back," she finished.

"It is strange how the strain persists, but indeed how could you be anything else?"

She smiled at him mockingly, then when his eyes met hers she suddenly felt shy.

She did not know why.

While she had remained unmoved by William and Lionel's compliments and those which had been accorded to her on the Continent, there was something in Vulcan's gaze which was different.

It made her feel young and not exactly embarrassed but shy, as a woman is with a man who is very masculine and to whom she responds not only with her mind but with her body.

It was something, she thought, that had never happened to her before and she lifted the hot tea to her lips to sip it, aware of its subtle fragrance even while she was vividly conscious of Vulcan watching her.

"You are lovely, unbelievably lovely!" he said. "How could I have guessed that here in England in the village in which I was born I would find exactly what I required for the very last picture in my book?"

"Will you show me the others?"

"Perhaps. But not to-day. I want you to think when you leave me that you are still portraying Persephone. I want to put your thoughts and feelings into my conception of what you are."

Astara smiled.

"Are you really suggesting I should think of nothing

else until I come to you again?"

"What else can be of any importance?" he enquired. "In completing my picture you are part of history, the history of the past and the history of the future."

"For the *Société de Géographes*?"

"Exactly!" he said, "and here in England, if it will interest you, the book will be published by the Association for Promoting the Discoveries of the Interior Parts of Africa."

Astara prevented herself from giving an exclamation, for her father had read papers at meetings of the Association on several occasions when they had persuaded him to speak of his travels in the African Continent.

"Where have you been in Africa?" she asked.

"To many places," Vulcan replied, "but you are to concentrate on Persephone and especially on Olympus which of course you know well."

"I have always had the feeling," Astara said, "that the reason why the gods and goddesses interfered so often with mortals is that they found that their gold tables on Olympus and celestial nectar and ambrosia palled after a time."

"I dare say you are right," he agreed, "and I am glad that my namesake had more active things to do."

"Of course you could always throw a thunderbolt," Astara smiled.

As she spoke she rose to her feet.

"Now I have to go."

"May I come with you?"

"No!"

"You promise to return?"

"I have given you my promise. I will not break it."

"Then, thank you," he said. "Thank you, Aphrodite, but when you have gone, I shall find it very hard to believe that you are real."

"Shall I say that I am as real as your picture?" Astara replied. "As real as the mysteries of Eleusis?"

"Then you are real, and you will come back to me," he said positively.

She walked across the room to pick up her bonnet.

She liked the manner in which he made no effort to join her as she walked towards the door.

He merely stood watching her. She turned to smile at him, but he did not respond and did not speak.

There was no sign of Chang but the front door was open.

Outside the Mill Astara felt the sun on her face and knew it was still warm but not as hot as it had been earlier in the day.

Then as she reached the turn in the road she started to run towards the wood.

She was not certain as she went whether she was running back to Worfield House or away from Vulcan.

CHAPTER FOUR

"You have not answered my question."

Astara started as William spoke, realising that she had been far away in her thoughts and had not heard what he said.

"I am sorry," she said. "I was day-dreaming."

"I hoped that you would be dreaming of me, but not when I am present."

There was a note of reproof in his tone and she knew that he was piqued because she had been absent-minded when he was talking to her and they were alone together.

They had finished dinner and Sir Roderick and Lionel had disappeared.

There was something in the way William spoke and the manner in which he was looking at her which told Astara uncomfortably he intended to propose to her.

She knew the signs only too well from the numbers of young men who, as Sir Roderick had said, had cast their hearts at her feet in Italy and in Paris.

"I wonder where Uncle Roderick is?" she asked. "I thought he was about to join us."

"I have no wish to have either my uncle or Lionel here at this moment," William replied. "I want to talk to you."

He reached out as he spoke and took her hands in his.

"I think, Astara," he began, "you know what I am going to say."

"No . . please," she murmured.

He thought she was shy and went on before she could say any more:

"I know we have not known each other for long, but we are both sensible enough to realise what my uncle wants. I assure you, Astara, that I want, more than I can possibly put into words, that you should become my wife."

Astara's fingers stiffened in his and she looked away from him towards the open window where the sun was just sinking in a golden glow and the stars were coming out overhead.

"I think we will be very happy here together," the Viscount continued, "our interests are the same, and I know, Astara, that I will make you happy."

He spoke with an obvious confidence and Astara knew that he was supremely sure of himself and of her answer.

"Please, William," she said after a moment, "do not . . say any more . . it is . . too soon . . much too soon for me to . . make up my mind."

"Then suppose you let me make it up for you? Or rather talk to Uncle Roderick? He is convinced that we are eminently suited to each other, but what is more important is that we should both of us be similarly sure of our future happiness."

He put out his arm to encircle Astara's waist, but as he did so she rose to her feet.

"It is . . too soon," she said.

As she spoke her eyes were drawn towards the picture over the mantelpiece.

She seemed to remember reading that all three of the goddesses had been confident that they would receive the apple from Paris, not through conceit in their beauty, but knowing that in addition what each had to offer him was of supreme importance.

She stood looking up at Hera remembering how she had said in an attempt to influence Paris's decision:

"If you will award the prize to me I will make you Lord over all Asia!"

That, Astara told herself, was what William was offering her.

Almost as if he read her thoughts he said:

"As my wife you will be able to entertain everybody of importance in London from the King, who has always given me his friendship, to the very cream of the *Beau Monde*."

He paused. Then as if his own imagination was excited by the prospect ahead he continued:

"You will be able to rival all the other great hostesses – the Duchess of Devonshire or Lady Bessborough – and we will see that the parties in our London house surpass them all!"

In a quiet voice Astara enquired:

"That is what you want?"

She did not turn her head but she was sure there was a smile on the Viscount's lips as he replied:

"There are many other things. I want to enlarge and improve my stable so that I can carry off the prizes at all the great races."

As if this suggested he was thinking only of himself he added hastily:

"I know that you are fond of horses and I think you can trust my judgement to find horses that you will enjoy riding and driving. And my coach-builders will make you the fastest and smartest curricle that has ever been seen in the Park."

He certainly put a good case for himself, Astara thought dispassionately.

He was waiting for an answer but when she did not speak he rose and came to stand just behind her.

"There are other things that will interest us both," he said, "but of course the most important is love."

He turned her round as he spoke and she saw that she had been right in thinking there was a smile on his lips.

There was also a certain glint in his eye and she questioned whether it was entirely one of love.

She could not help feeling that he had thrilled to his

own description of what their lives together could mean.

He put his arms around her. But when he bent his head to kiss her lips, moving smoothly with an expertise that she felt had something almost too professional about it, she freed herself and walked away towards the window.

"Astara!"

There was undoubtedly a note of surprise in William's exclamation.

"I have told you," she said. "It is too soon. We do not know each other well enough."

"I know you! I know you are everything I want – the woman who will bear my name and with whom I wish to spend the rest of my life."

He was too glib in the way he spoke, which Astara told herself grated on her, although perhaps she was being unreasonable and over-critical.

She stood looking out into the garden.

It was so beautiful, so romantic, and she thought that if she had been a man about to propose to a woman she would have made some excuse to take her outside and let the sinking sun and the twinkling stars speak far more eloquently than any words could do.

"You are being evasive, Astara," William said as he joined her at the window, "but I understand. Getting married is a very big step for a woman."

"As it is for a man?"

"Of course!" he answered. "But when a man finds the ideal person with whom he wishes to share his life, it is easy for him to make up his mind quickly and decisively."

"I appreciate that," Astara said, "and thank you for offering me the position of being your wife, but I still need more time to think about it."

"How long?"

She sensed the impatience behind the question and she smiled as she answered:

"What are a few hours, a few days, a few months, compared to the years we may spend in each other's company?"

"I will try to possess my soul in patience," William

said, "but do not keep me waiting too long."

He took her hand and raised it to his lips and as he did so to Astara's relief Sir Roderick and Lionel came into the Salon.

"You are looking at the stars?" Sir Roderick enquired as he crossed the room.

"It is very beautiful to-night, Uncle Roderick," Astara said, "and as you see, the sky is red – 'Red sky at night is a shepherd's delight!'"

She thought as she spoke that it would be fine to-morrow and therefore easy for her to go to Vulcan as she had promised to do.

She had no idea how it could be arranged without Sir Roderick being curious about her movements, but on one thing she was quite determined – she must not make William or Lionel suspicious that she was seeing their cousin.

She was sure that if she was wise she would tell Vulcan the truth about her identity, and tell him that lying on his desk was a very interesting invitation which could affect his whole life.

But she had the uncomfortable feeling that he might not be interested.

There was nothing about him to suggest that he was short of money and she was quite certain he had not written his book in order to make any.

"It is my turn to talk to you," Lionel said in her ear, "and you promised that I could teach you 'Piquet'."

"I have not forgotten," Astara replied, "so let me have my first lesson now. I am quite sure it is an accomplishment in which I am sadly lacking."

She realised that William was annoyed that she should move from his side with obviously no regrets.

She felt he was used to the type of woman who fawned on him and would not leave his side if there was a chance of their being together either alone or in company.

As she walked across the Salon to where at the end of it the servants had laid out a card-table and packs of cards, she knew that William's eyes were following her resentfully.

Sir Roderick, however, summed up the situation and engaged William in a conversation about horses.

Soon they were talking together by the fireside in a manner which precluded them, Astara knew, from hearing anything that she and Lionel said to each other.

She was not surprised when as they sat down at the table he shuffled the cards, then said:

"Shall I tell your fortune?"

"Are you a soothsayer?"

"Only where you are concerned."

"Then I think perhaps my fate should be left a secret until I meet a Gypsy. I am sure there were plenty at the Horse Fair who would have been able to predict my future."

"I can do that," he answered.

Astara looked amused and he said:

"You are standing at the cross-roads and you can go either right or left, but whichever way you turn it will be irrevocable and you will be unable to change your mind."

"Do you think I would wish to?"

"If you found you had made a mistake."

"I hope I shall not do that."

"It is very easy to do when someone is as lovely as you."

He spoke seriously as if he was not paying her a compliment but was really warning her.

"I love you, Astara!" he went on. "You are well aware of that, but I know I have little chance of your accepting me as a husband."

"Why should you say that?"

"Because I have always come off second best and that, I suppose, is what I shall continue to do."

"Are you referring to William?"

"Who else? I know what he was saying to you when we came into the room just now."

"Was it so obvious?"

"It was to me, and he has done everything possible to put me out of the running."

"How could he do that?"

Lionel smiled.

"I am not a sneak, Astara, nor would I try to win you in an unfair manner. But I love you and I think you are the most beautiful person I have ever seen in my life!"

"Thank you," Astara said, "but I do not think that beauty is really a foundation on which one can build a marriage. There is so much more to it than that."

Lionel thought for a moment, then he said:

"I think you are inferring that one should have brains, but I am not a brainy chap like the other Worfields."

He paused before he said:

"To tell the truth, my father was so clever and always trying to push me into being the same, that I hated everything they tried to make me learn at Eton."

"I can understand that," Astara said. "My father always said the most fatal thing where children are concerned is to try to force one's own enthusiasms on them."

"Your father was an understanding man. I used to go through agonies every term when I went home for the holidays knowing there would be a row as soon as I arrived over my school report."

"And the rows did not make you work any harder?"

"Of course not! It just made me dig my toes in and decide that knowledge – all knowledge – was a bore!"

Astara laughed.

"I can somehow see you defying your father and your teachers and putting a barrier between you and everything they wanted you to learn."

"You understand," Lionel said. "I assure you I suffered a great deal because of the cleverness of the Worfield family."

There was something boyish in the admission which made Astara say:

"I am really sorry for you."

"You cannot think what it was like," Lionel said,

"having first Uncle Roderick, then Uncle George held up to me as shining examples and, eventually of course, William."

"Is William clever?" Astara enquired.

"He was always the top of the form in one way or another."

"What do you mean by that?"

There was a little pause, then Lionel replied:

"Forget what I said."

"If you ask me to," Astara agreed. "So William was top not only at games – Uncle Roderick told me that – but also scholastically."

"He always went home with a prize," Lionel said, "but all I had to show of my progress were several extremely painful floggings!"

Astara laughed light-heartedly.

"Poor Lionel! You really make me sorry for you. At the same time I am sure you have made up for it since you grew up."

"I love being in the Regiment, but that does not prevent my father from shaking his head and saying he had hoped to have a son who would shine as he did in the political world."

"It would be impossible to have two orators in the family!" Astara laughed.

"That is what I have always thought myself," Lionel remarked, "and that brings us back to the beginning, Astara."

He looked across the table at her as he said with all sincerity:

"I cannot tell you in a lot of fancy words what I think about you. I can only say that I love you and it would be like reaching Heaven to be married to you. But I have a feeling you are not going to open the gates."

"It is too soon for me to make up my mind," Astara said firmly, "about anything."

"And when you do, it will undoubtedly be William," Lionel said with a sudden note of bitterness in his voice.

"I do not need to look at the cards of your hand to foresee that."

"I was thinking when I looked at the picture over the mantelpiece," Astara said, "that the three goddesses who appeared before Paris all attempted to influence his decision by offering him alluring promises."

Lionel looked towards the picture, but she could see it meant nothing to him.

"Athene," Astara went on, "promised Paris that he would always be victorious in battle."

"Did she, by Jove?" Lionel exclaimed. "That would be worth having, and I suppose by battle she did not only mean a fight on a battlefield."

"I think she meant," Astara explained, "that in everything he struggled to achieve he would finally be victorious."

"It is a pity that the goddess – what did you say her name was? – is not here now. She might have cast a magic spell on me so that I could win you."

"If you did I wonder if you would not find me somewhat of an encumbrance?" Astara suggested. "Soldiers are best when they are free."

"What makes you think that?"

"Well, supposing you were sent with your Regiment to some outlandish place? A wife and family would be restricting if nothing else."

"What you are saying is that I should have to make up my mind whether to leave you behind or subject you to the discomforts that most soldiers' wives have to endure."

Before Astara could reply he went on:

"One lucky thing is that it is extremely unlikely that the Life Guards would ever be sent to India or anywhere like that. I often have the feeling that we are more decorative than anything else."

"Your Regiment did very well at Waterloo, and it was there, I understand, that you were decorated."

"It was very exciting!" Lionel said and his eyes lit up. "I do not think I have ever been so thrilled by anything."

He saw that Astara was listening and after a moment he went on:

"Afterwards everyone talked about the slaughter, the horror, the men who died, and of course the Charge of the Scots Greys, but I like to remember the exhilaration I felt!"

There was a note of it in his voice and as Astara smiled he said:

"Perhaps because I was so young it never for a moment crossed my mind that we would not be victorious, but then who could fail not to believe in Wellington?"

The way he spoke, with a kind of hero-worship in his words and on his face, told Astara that that was really where his love lay – with his Regiment, the men he commanded and the General who commanded him.

She had the feeling, although she would not have said it aloud, that Lionel's wife would always take second place in his life and that he was really dedicated not to love but to war.

William put a stop to their conversation by deliberately rising from the fireplace and walking to the table.

"You do not seem to have got very far with your lesson," he said in a disagreeable tone.

"We were talking," Lionel replied defiantly.

"So I noticed," William said. "If it is a matter of conversation, then I should like to join in."

He pulled up a chair to seat himself at the table, but Astara rose.

"I am sure you are all tired after attending the Horse Fair," she said, "so I shall say good-night to you both and to Uncle Roderick and retire to bed."

"No, do not leave us!" William said sharply and she felt it was more of a command than a request.

She did not answer him but moved to Sir Roderick's side.

He looked up at her before he rose to his feet and she thought there was a question in his eyes.

She knew that with his sharp intelligence and perception where she was concerned, he would be aware that this evening she had received two proposals of marriage.

"Good-night, dear Uncle Roderick."

"Good-night, my dearest," he answered. "Sleep well and pleasant dreams."

"If I dream," Astara answered, "I hope it will be of the things which you and I have still to do together. You know that many of our plans are still incomplete."

For a moment there was a rueful expression on his face and she knew he was aware that she had refused, or at least had not accepted, both of his nephews.

Then as he kissed her cheek he quoted softly:

"Uncertain, coy, and hard to please!"

"That," Astara said firmly, "is one of the great advantages of being a woman."

She saw the twinkle come back into his eyes, then curtseyed gracefully to William and Lionel and left them alone in the Salon.

She found it impossible, however, to go to sleep at once.

Instead she lay thinking over the strange events of the day and her visit to Vulcan Worfield. The persistent question in her mind was how she could see him again.

She wanted to do so, there was no doubt about that. She found him intriguing and quite different from anything she had expected.

Who could have guessed for one moment that, while his relatives disparaged him for wandering aimlessly over the world, he was writing a book and painting pictures that she felt in their originality would arouse an almost violent controversy?

Because of her father she had a great respect for the Association for Promoting the Discovery of the Interior Parts of Africa.

Her father had spoken of it enthusiastically and she knew that it was a deliberate attempt to make the remote parts of the world more familiar to those who might never be able to travel except in their minds.

It was something her mother had said when she had begged her father to write down his experiences so that other people could enjoy them.

"Perhaps Astara will do that when she is older," he had replied.

"Why not?" her mother said. "At the same time I feel that the type of intellectual who will listen to you would never listen to a woman."

Now Vulcan was doing what her father had failed to do, and Astara knew that she would never rest until she had read his book and seen the rest of his pictures.

She was still undecided the following day as to how she could escape to Little Milden.

They all rode in the morning, then there was a luncheon party for the neighbours who had discovered that Sir Roderick was in residence. They had hurriedly called to inundate both him and Astara with invitations.

Sir Roderick, however, had avoided their hospitality by offering his own, and when they sat down twenty to luncheon Astara could see with amusement the expression of awe on the faces of the guests when they looked at him.

She had said to him once in Paris:

"You have an aura of gold about your head and to most people it is a sacred emblem."

He had laughed, but she knew he accepted that his wealth won for him a respect and almost a reverence wherever he might be.

After luncheon the guests wished to see the house and when at last they departed reluctantly the afternoon had almost gone.

"Let us go into the garden," William suggested to Astara.

She shook her head and when Sir Roderick joined them she said:

"You will think it tiresome of me, but I have a slight headache. I would like, if you do not need me to do anything for you, to lie down until dinner-time."

"Of course, my dear," Sir Roderick agreed.

He put his hand on her shoulder as he said:

"I thought at luncheon what a charming hostess you made at Worfield House. I am certain my nephews were thinking the same thing."

"You must remember," Astara said lightly, "that you made an exceptionally delightful host."

She knew as she walked away that he was amused at the adroit way she had turned his words.

When she reached her Bed-Room she quickly changed her gown from the elaborate one she had worn at luncheon and slipping down one of the side-staircases let herself out through a door which opened into the garden.

Because she was in a hurry to reach Vulcan she ran through the shrubberies which bordered the wood and soon found the path through the trees.

She was breathless by the time she reached Little Milden and only when she was actually in the village did she move more sedately and hope that her heart would cease beating so frantically.

The door of the Mill was open as she expected and she walked in to hear Vulcan's voice say sharply before he could see her:

"Is that you, Aphrodite? I thought you had forgotten your promise."

"I always keep my promises," she answered as she entered the big room.

He turned round from the easel to look at her and she suddenly became conscious that from her haste her hair was curling in small tendrils around her forehead and she was certain the colour was vivid in her cheeks.

She looked at him and looked away, then without waiting for instructions she walked to the throne and picked up the sheaf of wheat which was lying where she had left it.

She held it in her arms and assumed the pose that he wanted and looked up as if to the light.

He did not move for a moment, but she knew his eyes were on her. Then he said:

"Perfect! I see now where I have gone wrong."

He painted quickly and after some moments he said:

"Why did you have to run?"

"I . . thought you would be waiting for me."

"I was, but I have a fancy you have come quite a long way."

She did not answer and he smiled as he said:

"Still mysterious? Still intent on keeping me guessing?"

"Why not? Explanations are boring and often . . disappointing."

"Who told you that?" he questioned in an amused voice.

"Why should it not be my own observation?"

"Because you do not look as if you have ever been disappointed by anything in life."

"And how should one look if one was disappointed?"

"Cynical – but you are too young for that! Blasé – you are too ignorant. No – where youth scores every time is that you have hope and the imagination to be quite sure you will always get what you want."

"And what do I want?" Astara enquired.

"Love of course! Women never want anything else."

"And men?"

"Men have so many other things they need."

"Like money?" Astara asked.

"Money is unimportant in itself," Vulcan replied. "But it can aid ambition and achievement, and one can waste a whole lot of time finding how to pay for something one needs urgently."

"Is that what you have to do?"

"Sometimes I had to in the past."

"And now?"

"I have, thank God, everything I need from a financial point of view, but money is not my main objective."

"Of course not! You want your book and your pictures to be a success."

"They will be!"

"How can you be sure that people will understand?"

"People? Who concerns himself with people?" he asked. "I am speaking of the few – the very few who will understand and will know what I am trying to say."

"That is what I wanted to ask you .. what are you trying to say?"

He did not reply and she asked:

"You have not yet told me what your book is about except that it concerns the mystery of Eleusis."

"That is not the only mystery in the world."

"Are you saying you are writing a book of mysteries?"

"Briefly – yes!"

"How exciting! What other ones do you include?"

"Mecca."

Astara was so surprised that she turned her face to look at him.

"Are you telling me that you have been as a pilgrim to Mecca?" she asked incredulously.

"Yes!"

"I can hardly believe it!"

She had heard her father talk of the pilgrimage that Moslems made to what to them was the secret city of Islam, the holy of holies, which was eight days' march across the torrid Arabian desert.

She also knew that no infidel could penetrate the city and live.

Her father had told Astara that many attempts had been made by explorers and Christians to reach the Holy City, but they had never returned to tell what they had seen and discovered.

"H . how . . . did you get there?" Astara asked now.

"It was not a particularly pleasant journey," Vulcan answered lightly, "but you see before you a Master of Sufi, one of the Faithful, and entitled to a green turban!"

Astara almost gasped out that she wished she could tell her father about it. Then she questioned:

"And you have painted a picture of it?"

"Yes, but it does not really do it credit. The mysteries, the secrecy and the faith that vibrate around the Ka'ba, the sacred black shrine, are indescribable!"

Astara gave a little sigh.

"I wish I could see it!"

"That is definitely something you will never do," Vulcan smiled, "and as a matter of fact I have almost decided not to include that mystery in my book or exhibit the picture."

"Why not?"

"Because I might want to go back. I hope to visit many Moslem countries, and if it was known that I had deceived them not only should I be restricted but my life would be forfeit."

Astara knew that restriction was a word that mattered to him.

"It seems a pity to waste the experience," she said. "At the same time I think I understand."

"That I do not wish to be restricted?"

"Yes."

"I doubt it," he said. "Women never understand such things. They want to tie a man down, fetter him, and keep him in a cage."

"Not all women," Astara said, thinking of her mother.

"All women!" Vulcan said firmly. "And if a prodigy exists who does not feel like that, I have not met her."

He looked at Astara as he spoke. Then with a note of amusement in his voice he said:

"Of course, if she was a goddess like Aphrodite she might be different."

Astara did not know why, but his words depressed her. She could almost feel him moving away from her, disappearing into the desert disguised as a Moslem, wearing the green turban to which he was entitled, and she would never see him again.

"What are you thinking?" Vulcan asked suddenly.

"Of you crossing the desert," Astara answered truthfully, "under a sky terrible in its stainless beauty and the splendours of a pitiless blinding glare."

"So they have a Library on Olympus!" Vulcan remarked.

He painted for some minutes in silence. Then Astara asked:

"What other mysteries are there in your book?"

"The dance of the Dervishes."

"You . . have seen . . that?"

"It was fantastic, horrible, and yet mesmeric."

"I wish I could have been with you."

"It was not a sight for a woman or for anyone with a queazy stomach."

"May I see the picture?"

"Perhaps. You are making me nervous with your pose of understanding. I do not like being understood."

"I am sorry. I will look vacant and idiotic. Perhaps that will please you."

Astara spoke scathingly and now he put down his brush and turned round to look at her.

"Damn you!" he said. "I lay awake last night thinking about you. You are disturbing as well as intriguing me, and I do not like it!"

"The solution is quite simple."

"If you are going to say that you will stay away and not return, I think I shall strike you!"

"Why?"

"Because I want you here. You know I want you here! But you are too much for one man's peace of mind!"

Astara could hear her heart beating and she knew that what he was saying and the tone in which he said it made her feel breathless.

"You are very difficult to please, Mr Worfield," she said at length.

"Not really," he answered. "It is only that I am unused to perfection and I am finding it hard to adjust myself to it."

He was still looking at her as he said as if to himself:

"There must be a flaw somewhere!"

His eyes swept over her from the top of her head to her feet. Then he turned back to his easel.

"Doubtless," he said in a mocking voice, "the answer

is that you have a husband and six children hidden away somewhere."

"And I can still manage to look like Persephone?"

He laughed.

"I will concede you that point. But do not forget she must have had some erotic experiences with Pluto in Hades."

"I believe that she was clever enough to keep him at arms' length," Astara answered, "and to tell him she would consider what he suggested next winter . . then the next . . then the next . ."

"Is that what you would do?"

It was, Astara thought with amusement, exactly what she was doing – keeping William and Lionel at arms' length.

"You will have to marry sooner or later," Vulcan said and the statement made her start.

"Why should you say that?"

"Because I feel that is what you are considering. Women have to marry. There is no other way open for them."

"You did not think so where . . Moll was concerned."

"You are rather different from Moll, and I cannot imagine that the young man who is asking you to marry him is a traveller in fancy goods!"

"No . . he is not . . that."

"What is he then?"

"A gentleman of many talents."

"Are you in love with him?"

The question was sharp and while Astara considered what she should reply Vulcan said:

"There is no need to answer. I know that you have never been in love!"

"H . how do you . . know that?"

"By looking at you. By being aware of what you are thinking and feeling. Your innocence protects you far more effectively than any armour could do."

Astara was so surprised that she dropped her pose to look at him.

"How can you . . know such things?"

"Perhaps my initiation into many mysteries has made me more perceptive than most people."

"Into how many have you been initiated?"

"We were talking about you!"

"I thought rather we were talking about your travels and the things you have seen and done."

"I have no wish to talk about myself, and now as I suspect your sheaf is feeling heavy you can get down for a moment. I want you to look at my picture."

"Very well."

She put down the sheaf as he suggested and walked from the dais to the easel.

She saw at once that he had done a great deal to the picture since yesterday.

Now Persephone stood out almost like a pillar of light; in fact the light seemed almost to be centred in her and come from her.

She was painted in a strange way that Astara had never seen before, but she knew it was meant to evoke emotion rather than to portray an image.

"Do you like it?" he asked.

"Do I really look like that?"

"Better in many ways. I find it hard to show how unsure you are within yourself."

Astara looked at him with startled eyes.

"Unsure?" she questioned.

He looked at her and her eyes were held by his as he said:

"I feel as if you are being pushed to the edge of a precipice. You are afraid, and yet at the same time you feel that what you have to do is inevitable."

"And what . . do I have to . . do?"

"I have no crystal ball by which I can read the future," Vulcan answered, "but if you wish me to guess, I imagine you will do what you are expected to do."

"Why should I do that?"

"Because you are a woman, because I doubt if there is an alternative."

"And if there . . was?"

"Then – I think you might take it. There is something in you as yet undeveloped which would make you less compliant than most people might think"

"That is what I . . want to be!" she said passionately, "but you are right . . I am afraid!"

He was still as if he was undecided about something, then he walked to the wall where a number of canvasses stood.

He turned one round and she saw it depicted vividly, almost violently, the dance of the Dervishes.

The painting was done in a way that made one feel rather than see what was happening: the unrestrained movements of their hypnotised bodies, the howling of their voices, the bared teeth, the extended nostrils, the dilated eyes.

It was horrible, and yet as he had said mesmeric.

"Is it what you expected?" Vulcan asked.

"From . . you? Yes!" Astara replied.

He turned round another canvas.

Here was something quite different: the peace and quiet and strange symbolism of a Zen Buddhist garden, the raked white gravel in rhythmic lines, the stones which depicted the river of life and the reincarnation of man.

There was a serenity and again a strange light which made Astara think she saw what was not actually there, but rather in her mind.

"You have studied Zen Buddhism?" she asked.

"So you knew that is what it is?" he parried.

She nodded.

She thought he looked at her curiously before he turned round yet another picture.

This depicted a sacrifice in the Temple of Kali: the blood of the slaughtered animals, the stench, and the lustful participation of the worshippers were almost too vivid, too unpleasant to look at for more than a moment.

As if he understood what he had made her feel Vulcan put the canvas back and said:

"That is enough for now. As you see there are half-a-dozen more which I will show to you another time, so my picture of Mecca will not be missed."

"I want to see them all!" Astara insisted, but Vulcan shook his head.

"The light is going and I must finish your picture."

"And after that?" she asked.

"I shall take it to the engravers. The others have already been done."

He spoke in an absent-minded way and she knew he was already engrossed with his painting.

She stepped back onto the dais and picked up the sheaf of wheat.

She wondered what he felt about her.

She had the feeling that when this last picture was complete he would have no interest in anything that he had already done and accomplished, but only in what lay in the future.

He was a strange man and different from anyone she had ever met before.

Yet in a way there was something familiar about him, something that she recognised though it seemed intangible, which was comprehensible in the same manner that she understood what he was trying to say in his pictures.

She knew that he was right when he said they were painted only for the few and Astara wondered if even Sir Roderick would appreciate them.

She knew he preferred a more conventional type of painting, the Rubens, the Van Dykes, the Leonardo Da Vincis which they had seen on their travels.

He had excellent taste, but it was a taste that was based on what was accepted by the experts, and she was quite certain that Vulcan's work would not fit into that category.

And yet, she told herself, there would be certain people like her father who would have acclaimed it as a new type of art which would bring a new sort of understanding to those who searched for it.

Deep in her thoughts she must have stood for a long time without realising she was doing so. Suddenly Vulcan said:

"I have finished! To do any more would be a mistake."

"Really finished?" Astara asked.

"Come and see for yourself!"

She obeyed him and she thought that the whole picture seemed to blaze with the light that came from Persephone – while she in her turn evoked something beyond herself, something she looked for in the sky.

It was uncanny, and yet brilliant, what he had managed to convey with a brush-stroke, and a touch of light where one least expected it.

She was silent for so long that at last Vulcan said:

"Tell me! I want to hear."

"There are .. no words," Astara answered in a low voice, "but it makes me a .. part of it .. and yet it is a part .. of me."

"That is what I wanted."

He looked at the picture, then at the others lying against the wall.

"As soon as this one is engraved," he said, "I shall take them all to Paris. Are you coming with me?"

She looked up at him, feeling she could not have heard him aright and saw his lips smiling and there was an expression in his eyes that held her spellbound.

"That will be a new experience for you," he said, "and one I want to give you."

He put his arms round her as he spoke and drew her to him, and his mouth came down on hers.

Vaguely, a long way away at the very back of her mind, she thought she ought to resist him, but it was too late.

His lips held her completely captive and she knew that this was what she wanted; this was why she had been waiting.

She felt a strange, unaccountable sensation rise through her body, through her breasts and up her throat.

It was as if her whole being moved to become part of him.

She felt too as if they were both enveloped in a blinding light – the light that was in the pictures, the light that came from Persephone, the light of the gods.

It was so wonderful, so unexpected, and yet in a way so sacred that she felt as if she was revitalised and reborn in the light, and yet it was Vulcan's arms, his lips and him.

He held her closer and still closer.

His mouth moved a little and she thought he would set her free, but he merely kissed her more insistently, more demandingly, and she felt as if she and he became indivisible and she was no longer herself.

Finally, after what might have been an hour, or a century, he raised his head and looked down at her face, his eyes searching hers as if he sought for something, though she was not certain what it was.

Then she knew he had found it and he was kissing her again.

Kissing her until her feet were no longer on the ground, until she touched the stars, the light that came from the sun and the moon and she was not human but divine.

At last he raised his head and because she was so bewildered, bemused and dazzled by him she could only hide her face against his shoulder and feel that if he took his arms from her she would fall down on the ground at his feet.

"My sweet! My little Aphrodite!" he said in a hoarse voice. "You have come into my life and I can never let you go!"

A ripple of sunshine was flooding through Astara and as she felt his lips on her hair, she raised her face to say:

"I love . . you!"

The words were very faint, and there was a note of astonishment in them as if they were too wonderful and too incredible even to be spoken.

"That is what I want to hear," Vulcan said, "and now,

my darling, everything is very simple and there need be no more mysteries between us."

Astara forced herself to try and think clearly.

She had been kissed and become part of a man who did not even know her name and had no idea who she was!

A man who had asked her to go with him to Paris having, as was obvious from what he had said before, no intention of offering her marriage.

In a voice that did not seem to be her own, she said:

"I . . must go back . . but I . . promise that I will . . come and see you . . tomorrow and then . . perhaps we can . . make plans."

She felt as if every word was difficult to utter.

Her whole being was throbbing with the sensations he had aroused in her – the room was filled with strange music, and she could hardly make herself heard above it.

"I will go to London very early," Vulcan said, "and be back at about this time. Then, as you say, we can make plans."

"I . . must . . go now," Astara murmured.

"Why?" he asked, and he was kissing her again passionately, demandingly.

She felt as if he took her mind as well as her body and made it his.

It was impossible to think of anything but the sensations that once again rose in her, leaving her breathless, at the same time throbbing with an ecstasy that was not only physical but spiritual.

Only when his lips released her did she manage to say:

"I . . I must . . go . . p . please . . do not . . stop me."

"I would never do anything you did not wish," he replied, "but I want you, Aphrodite, God how much I want you!"

He would have taken her in his arms again but she put up her hands to stop him, feeling that he swept her along like a tidal wave and she would find it impossible not to do anything he asked of her.

"P . please . ." she pleaded.

The word came instinctively to her lips. She had not even thought that she must say it.

"Very well," he agreed. "I will let you go if you must, but you will be back to-morrow? Promise me, or I shall have to take you with me to London."

"I . . I . . promise," Astara managed to reply.

She had moved a little way from him when he said:

"Come here!"

She turned her head irresolutely, afraid of his power over her, and yet longing to obey him.

"I . . I . . must . . go!"

"I told you to come here!"

She looked into his eyes and was lost.

Without meaning to, she was back in his arms and he was kissing her again, kissing her as if he was determined to take possession of her, to demand from her not only her body but her soul.

Only when she had ceased to think and there was only a wild rapture that made her want him to go on kissing her for ever did he let her go.

"First things first!" he said, and his voice was unsteady. "I shall be counting the seconds, my little goddess, until to-morrow evening."

Because she knew she dare not stay any longer Astara turned and ran from the room.

Only as she reached the outside door did she lean against it for a moment to catch her breath and force herself to realise that she was back on earth – a human being with very human problems.

CHAPTER FIVE

Astara started to come down the Grand Staircase the next morning and as she did so she saw that Sir Roderick was below in the Hall talking to Mr. Barnes.

"Very well," she heard him say, "I will see those men to-morrow morning at nine o'clock. It will mean I shall have to ride later, but I suppose it is urgent?"

"They are very anxious, Sir Roderick, for you to pass the plans so that they can put the work in hand," Mr. Barnes replied.

"Very well," Sir Roderick said. "Nine o'clock, and tell them not to be late."

He moved away towards the Dining-Room and Mr. Barnes picking up his hat walked towards the front door.

He had just reached the steps outside when Astara had an idea.

"Mr. Barnes!" she called and started to run down the stairs.

The Agent stopped and looked back at her. Then when he would have re-entered the house she joined him and walked outside ahead of him, into the sunshine.

When they were out of hearing of the footmen in attendance in the Hall, Astara said:

"I wonder, Mr. Barnes, if you would do something for me?"

"Of course, Miss Beverley," he replied. "Anything that is within my capabilities."

He smiled as he spoke and Astara knew that he admired her, for there was no mistaking the expression in his eyes.

"It is something which concerns Sir Roderick . . ." she began.

She hesitated, then went on:

"I know, although he will not say so, that he is very upset that his nephew, Mr. Vulcan, who lives in Little Milden has not been to see him."

"I thought it rather strange myself," Mr. Barnes said, "but then I believe Mr. Vulcan is a law unto himself."

"I have heard that, too," Astara replied, "and Captain Lionel tells me that it is well known he seldom answers letters if he bothers to open them!"

"Do you mean Sir Roderick wrote to him?" Mr. Barnes asked.

"Yes, he wrote," Astara answered. "But Mr. Vulcan has not replied nor come to see his uncle. I can only surmise that he has in fact not read the letter."

"Then what would you like me to do, Miss Beverley?" Mr. Barnes enquired.

"I wonder," Astara said choosing her words carefully, "if without mentioning it to Sir Roderick you could go to see Mr. Vulcan and tell him that his uncle is . . hurt by his behaviour and his . . negligence."

She thought Mr. Barnes looked uncomfortable as if he thought it was a difficult assignment and went on quickly:

"I feel sure once he understands that Sir Roderick is getting old and is anxious to see him, he will call at Worfield House."

"I am sure he would," Mr. Barnes agreed.

Astara thought that his tone did not sound over-confident but she smiled and said:

"Do try to persuade him to come to dinner to-night."

"I will do my best, Miss Beverley," Mr. Barnes promised.

"That would be very kind of you," Astara said, "and

please, do not mention me to Mr. Vulcan or tell Sir Roderick that I said anything to you about his nephew. I would not like it to . . look as if I was . . interfering."

"No, of course not. I understand," Mr. Barnes replied.

Astara gave him a dazzling smile and went back into the house.

When breakfast was over and Sir Roderick informed them all that he would be ready to ride in a quarter-of-an-hour she slipped round to the stables.

Sam, the head-groom, who admired the way she rode, was always ready to do anything she asked of him.

Astara handed him a piece of paper which she had sealed with a wafer.

"I should be very grateful, Sam, if you would send the same groom who visited Mr. Vulcan Worfield's house in Little Milden last week, with this note. Tell him to put it through the door as he did before."

Sam took the piece of paper from her, looked at it in surprise, but being a well-trained servant said nothing.

"And please do not mention it to Sir Roderick," Astara said, "because if you do it will spoil a surprise."

"Oi'll say nothin' if ye asks Oi not to, Miss," Sam replied.

"Thank you, Sam," Astara said, "and send the groom soon."

"Oi'll do that, Miss, soon as ye've gone a-riding."

Astara went back to the house hoping that her plans would not go awry.

She had lain awake all night wondering what she should do about Vulcan, and she knew that he must now learn who she was, and most important, what Sir Roderick required.

She knew that she loved him overwhelmingly and that the emotions he had aroused in her and the ecstasy that she had felt when he kissed her were something vouchsafed to few people.

It had been so perfect that there were no words to describe it.

At the same time, even if he had felt the same ecstasy as he had given her, that was not to say he would wish to marry her!

He had made it very plain what he thought about marriage.

She was certain he was speaking the truth when he said he did not wish to be restricted or constrained.

Where then was there a place for her in his life?

She was afraid of the answer to that question and she could only hide her face in her pillow and say over and over again:

"I love you! I love you!"

When dawn came, having slept very little, Astara rose from her bed to pull back the curtains and look out at the beauty of the mist rising from the lake and the sunshine on the trees in the park.

Would any ordinary man, she asked herself, be willing to leave such loveliness for some far-off horizon?

But Vulcan was not ordinary and perhaps Sir Roderick was right in thinking he had a wanderlust which would never be assuaged.

She remembered how her father had found it impossible to settle down for long. But his life in a small house in the small village was very different from that of the owner of Worfield House and its vast Estates.

Here there would always be something to occupy Vulcan and stimulate his mind. But would it be enough?

Astara felt almost as if the question was asked out loud and she turned from the window to look to where on her dressing-table there stood a picture of her mother.

It was only a miniature painted by some unimportant artist when they were on their travels, but it had caught not only the sweetness of Charlotte Beverley's expression but the light of adventure in her eyes and the smile of happiness on her lips.

"Help me, Mama! Help Vulcan to realise that he would be happy with me as Papa was with you."

Even as she spoke Astara thought it was a vain prayer

which would go unheard.

Vulcan was very different from her father, even though in some ways they were alike.

She had the feeling that Vulcan was driven by stronger forces than her father had been, and the manner in which he had concentrated on his pictures made her afraid for herself.

She had the feeling that nothing would turn him aside from his chosen path, nothing would be allowed to intervene between him and what had aroused his interest.

For a man of such vibrant personality could love ever be anything of great importance?

Astara moved restlessly about her Bed-Room.

For the first time since she had slept at Worfield House its beauty and its luxury meant nothing to her.

All she wanted was to be with Vulcan, whether it was in a tent in the desert, a cave in the mountains, or trekking for miles uncomfortably on a wild mule or bad-tempered camel.

"I love him! I love him!" she cried despairingly.

But she felt that her voice was smothered in the silk hangings of the bed, in the softness of the carpet and in the beauty of the painted ceiling.

Then as if she could not face reality but wanted only to return to her dreams, she got back into bed and shutting her eyes recaptured the sensations she had felt when Vulcan kissed her.

She felt herself thrill and thrill again to the wonder of his lips, the closeness of his arms and the deepness of his voice.

She had seen the fire in his eyes and she knew that she aroused him and that he had spoken the truth when he said he wanted her.

But how much? And for how long?

She had found it difficult at breakfast to talk brightly of commonplace things with William and Lionel.

They were both looking exceedingly handsome in their riding-clothes, their boots polished until they reflected like mirrors the objects around them, their cravats masterpieces of fashion and style.

But Astara's mind kept returning to the plans that she had made for Vulcan to dine to-night at Worfield House.

She hoped he would be disappointed when he saw what she had written on the piece of paper that the groom would carry to Little Milden.

"I cannot come to-day, but will be with you the first thing in the morning.

Aphrodite."

If he was disappointed, he might more easily agree to Mr. Barnes' suggestion that he should make his uncle happy by dining to-night at Worfield House.

Astara had taken pains to disguise her hand-writing in case he should compare it with the letter which was still lying unopened on his desk.

Perhaps now that he had taken his pictures to London he would be prepared to open the letters that awaited him and deal with them.

She had a feeling that because he was so astute and perceptive he would guess who she was, and she wondered what she could do if he refused in consequence to come to Worfield House.

She was suddenly beset by a terrifying fear that rather than meet her again as Sir Roderick's Ward he would leave immediately for Paris.

She wanted to cry aloud at the idea.

Then she remembered that before he left England he would have to wait for her picture to be engraved in London so that he could take it with him.

At the same time, even if he did not go at once to Paris, he still might leave Little Milden.

"What is the matter, Astara? You look worried!"

It was Lionel who asked the question.

She thought it was typical of the two cousins that it should be Lionel who noticed her feelings while she was certain that William was only concerned with his own.

"The matter? Why should anything be the matter?" Sir Roderick asked before Astara could reply. "You are not ill?"

"No, of course not!" Astara replied. "I am greatly looking forward to our ride. We are so lucky to have such wonderful weather. I see the newspapers say that it is the warmest April there has been for twenty years!"

Her words diverted Sir Roderick's attention and he began to talk of Aprils he had known in the past when there had been frost and unseasonable showers of hail.

When she was once mounted on her horse it was easy for Astara to think without drawing attention to herself.

She thought she had never known a day to pass so slowly, and by tea-time she was longing almost uncontrollably to slip away through the wood to Little Milden and see if Vulcan had returned from London.

It was six o'clock when one of the footmen came to her side when she was seated in the Salon to say that Mr. Barnes would like a word with her.

She rose quickly to her feet and went out into the Hall to find him waiting.

"I thought you would like to know, Miss Beverley," Mr. Barnes said, "that Mr. Vulcan has agreed to dine with Sir Roderick to-night and will be here just before seven-thirty!"

"Thank you, Mr. Barnes, it was very kind of you to speak to him and also to let me know."

"He seemed surprised to hear that Sir Roderick was in residence. I often think Little Milden, although it is in fact so near, is cut off from us by the wood, as if we were in another county."

"I thought that must be the explanation why Mr. Vulcan had not called on his uncle," Astara said, "and I know Sir Roderick will be very pleased to see him."

"I am sure he will, Miss Beverley," Mr. Barnes agreed.

Astara thanked him again and ran up the staircase to her Bed-Room.

She knew that her heart was beating excitedly and she

felt an irrepressible excitement not only at the thought of seeing Vulcan again but of meeting him as herself.

At the same time she knew as she bathed and chose her most attractive gown that she was nervous and a little afraid.

Supposing he was angry when he found she had deceived him?

Supposing the deception killed the feeling that existed between them, the magic that was more compelling than anything she had ever imagined was possible?

"I love him!" she said again in her heart as she looked at her mother's portrait.

She knew now why her mother had refused the brilliant and wealthy Roderick Worfield for the obscure and poor Charles Beverley.

Astara found it strange to remember that if her mother had accepted her more important suitor, this house and Estate would have been hers by right of inheritance.

There would be no need for his three nephews to be considered as he was considering them now.

Then, Astara told herself, her choice could have been a very much wider one, but she was sure that Sir Roderick would keep his promise and not force her to marry any man whom she did not love.

At the same time he would undoubtedly be disappointed that it should not be William.

He had made his preference for the Viscount very obvious and he never missed an opportunity of pointing out to her how outstanding he was and how well he would fill the position as owner of Worfield House.

But Astara knew that neither William nor Lionel, much as she liked them, would ever evoke in her the rapture that she had known when Vulcan kissed her.

Even before he had done so, she had been vividly aware of his personality and of the strange aura which seemed to emanate from him.

It drew her in a way in which she had never been drawn to a man before.

"Have you ever been in love, Emma?" she asked the maid who was fastening her gown.

Emma was an apple-cheeked country-girl who had lived on the Worfield Estate all her life and had been taught her duties by the Head Housemaid who had been at Worfield House for nearly thirty years.

"Yes, Miss," Emma answered, and blushed as she spoke.

"Are you in love at the moment?" Astara enquired.

"Yes, Miss."

"And it makes you happy?"

"Oh, yes, Miss. It's ever so nice!" Emma answered.

Astara smiled.

Emma might find love "ever so nice", but she felt it was not only an ecstasy but a pain.

As she went downstairs she knew that there was a conflict within her that made her feel as if her whole body was a battlefield.

She entered the Salon to find Sir Roderick and William already there.

They were standing talking intently at the far end of the room and she had a feeling that what they were saying concerned her.

As she moved towards them there was that expression on their faces which people always assume when they are trying to look at their ease, while feeling a little uncomfortable because the subject of their conversation has interrupted them.

Sir Roderick was looking as usual extremely smart in his evening clothes. He always looked particularly distinguished when dressed for dinner as Astara had told him many times when they were in Europe.

However elegant, however important the other man in the party might be, Sir Roderick always appeared to outshine them.

There was no doubt too that William was looking his best.

He wore one large black pearl stud in the front of his

evening shirt, the points of his collar above his cravat reached to his chin and his black pantaloons strapped under the sole of his foot in the manner invented by the Prince Regent were a triumph of the tailor's art.

Astara knew by the expression in William's eyes that she too was looking attractive.

Her gown of white with small diamanté embroidered on it made her look more ethereal than usual.

She had taken a great deal of trouble with her hair and its burnished sheen seemed almost as brilliant as the exquisite little diamond brooches that her maid had set amongst the curls.

There were diamonds round her neck and round her wrists.

She had known as she chose them that she was deliberately showing Vulcan that she was not the village maiden he had first supposed her to be but definitely a goddess in her own sphere.

The door opened and Astara looked round quickly, but it was Lionel who came into the room.

"You are looking very smart this evening, Astara!" he said as he joined the gentlemen standing by the mantelpiece. "Are we expecting guests?"

Astara was just wondering what she would reply when the door opened again and the Butler announced:

"Mr. Vulcan Worfield, Sir!"

Sir Roderick looked round in surprise.

As Vulcan came into the room Astara found it hard to look at him.

She felt as if her eyes had become unfocused and her whole being was so tense that he walked towards them in a mist.

Then she saw that he looked different from the way he had before and realised it was because it was the first time she was seeing him without his painter's smock.

At the back of her mind she had been half-afraid that he would come wearing the unconventional clothes that he doubtless assumed on his travels.

She knew if he did it would be easy for William to make fun of him after he had gone, or perhaps to sneer at him in a lofty fashion.

But Vulcan was quite conventionally garbed, in fact his cravat was as well tied as either of his cousins' and his clothes fitted him just as elegantly.

The difference, Astara thought, was that he gave the impression of being supremely unconscious that they were of any importance.

"Vulcan, my dear boy!" Sir Robert exclaimed. "This is a delightful surprise!"

"You must forgive me, Uncle Roderick, for not calling on you sooner," Vulcan replied, "but to tell the truth I have been so busy that it was only to-day I opened your letter."

"Better late than never!" Sir Roderick exclaimed. "I cannot tell you how glad I am to see you!"

"And I to see you!" Vulcan answered. "I think it must be four years since we last met."

"Nearer five," Sir Roderick replied, "and I almost despaired of ever catching up with you again!"

"Well, I am here now," Vulcan smiled, "and it's nice to think that you are in England, and Worfield House is open."

"As it will always be to you," Sir Roderick answered. "But now, let me introduce you to my Ward!"

Astara's eyes had been on Vulcan's face all the time he was talking to Sir Roderick, and now as it seemed that he noticed her for the first time, she felt the colour rise in her cheeks.

He was completely composed and she knew she had been right in thinking that when he read the letter she had written on Sir Roderick's instructions he had realised who she was.

He bowed and she curtsied. Then Sir Roderick was saying:

"Your two cousins are here, as you see. Both William and Lionel were certain as you did not reply to my letter that you must be in some far-off part of the Globe."

"No, I was only at Little Milden," Vulcan replied. "How are you, William?"

He nodded to William, then held out his hand to Lionel.

"We have not met for a very long time," he said, "but I heard that you were decorated at Waterloo. Many congratulations!"

"I was lucky," Lionel answered.

"I envied you," Vulcan said. "It must have been a great experience."

"It was!" Lionel replied.

His eyes lit up as if he was pleased that Vulcan understood what it had meant to him.

"I thought you were beach-combing somewhere on the Equator!" William said in a supercilious manner. "The last time I heard of your exploits you were on a cargo ship bound for the East Coast of Africa."

"That was some years ago," Vulcan answered. "It proved to be quite an interesting journey."

"I shall want to hear all about it, my dear boy," Sir Roderick said, "but before we start reminiscing, let me suggest a glass of champagne."

The footmen were already in the room pouring the wine into crystal glasses which only Astara refused.

With his glass in his hand Vulcan looked up at the picture over the mantelpiece. Astara watched him, wondering what his reaction would be.

He stared at it for some seconds, then she saw a twinkle in his eyes and knew without saying so, that he understood the inner meaning behind the letter he had received from his uncle.

"'The Judgement of Paris'," he said aloud. "I have always liked Van Aachen's paintings."

"It is Astara's favourite," Sir Roderick said. "There is no doubt that he was a great technician, but it is not really to my taste."

Astara waited for Vulcan's reply. Then he said:

"I think he portrays more successfully than most what lies beneath the surface."

Astara felt her heart give a little leap.

He did understand! He did know why she liked that picture better than the others of more repute which hung round the walls.

As if he knew what she was feeling Vulcan turned and looked at her.

Just for a moment everyone else in the room vanished, they were alone and she was close to him.

Then as Astara was unable to do, he looked away and said:

"I see you have acquired some new pictures, Uncle Roderick. I shall look forward to your telling me about them."

"There will be plenty of time for that," Sir Roderick replied, "but now dinner is ready."

It was a strange meal, Astara thought, as they sat in the big Dining-Room making, because they were such a small party, a little island of light.

She found it almost impossible to eat, and was acutely aware of the undercurrents of feeling around the table.

Because of Sir Roderick's obvious delight at seeing Vulcan and the interest he was showing in him William was clearly annoyed while Lionel was, Astara knew, watching her almost apprehensively.

She thought that because he loved her, he sensed that she had an interest in Vulcan which was far from normal towards a man to whom she had only just been introduced.

She tried to hide her feelings, and yet it was impossible not to find her eyes continually drawn to Vulcan's face, not to listen intently to everything he was saying.

She felt as if they vibrated magnetically to each other across the table.

Astara was sitting on Sir Roderick's right while Vulcan was on the left. William was on the other side and Lionel next to Vulcan.

As if he was determined that she should attend to him William said in a commanding manner:

"I want to talk to you after dinner."

"What about?" Astara enquired.

"I will tell you when we are alone."

She did not reply and because she thought William was being rather tiresome, she deliberately turned to join in the conversation which Sir Roderick was having with Vulcan.

To her astonishment she heard Sir Roderick say:

"You must tell me, dear boy, in detail about Harrar."

Astara looked at him in surprise as Sir Roderick continued:

"I am told no white man has ever entered it and lived."

"Do you mean . . Harrar in . . Abyssinian Somaliland?" Astara exclaimed. "But you cannot have been there!"

Her father had told her about Harrar many years ago.

It was the centre, he had said, of the East African slave trade as well as a seat of Moslem culture.

Strange and mysterious legends abounded about the impregnable city, but although it was a place her father had longed to visit her mother had dissuaded him because even to attempt to enter Harrar was incredibly dangerous.

"Who told you I have been to Harrar?" Vulcan asked Sir Roderick.

"I have my ways of knowing these things," his uncle replied.

"I suppose knowing you I should not be surprised," Vulcan said. "But I am!"

"Personally, I think it was rather foolhardy of you to attempt such a journey," Sir Roderick said, "but I suppose it was no more dangerous than going to Mecca."

Vulcan threw back his head and laughed.

"Uncle Roderick, you are incorrigible! And the best-informed man in the world!"

"You forget that you are a relation, and I have always been very interested in my relations, though I have not seen as much of them as I might have done."

If Vulcan was surprised so was Astara.

Sir Roderick had said Vulcan was a drifter, a wanderer. How could he reconcile that with the incredible bravery of a man who had achieved the impossible, who had made the pilgrimage to Mecca and penetrated the secrecy of Harrar?

"I myself find all this bogey-bogey about secret cities and mysterious shrines boring and in most cases exaggerated," William remarked. "What good do such journeys do anyone, least of all yourself?"

Astara thought that Vulcan would tell his cousin how interested the Association in England and the *Société* in Paris were in what he had achieved.

Instead he replied:

"I am looking forward, William, to hearing of your adventures on the turf. Topsail was certainly a popular winner in Little Milden!"

"I thought it would give the locals something to talk about," William said complacently. "Did you back him yourself?"

"To tell the truth, I forgot to do so," Vulcan replied.

Seeing the supercilious smile on William's lips Astara knew that he thought the real reason why Vulcan had abstained was that he could not afford it.

She wondered if Sir Roderick would notice the cut and thrust between the two cousins, and then was sure that he was well aware of it.

She wondered if William's obvious antipathy to Vulcan was due to her.

Then she told herself it might in part be the fact that Vulcan looked so outstanding, so different in a way that was difficult to explain from his two cousins.

Conventionally dressed, as elegant as they were, there should have been little outward difference between them.

Yet as far as she was concerned Vulcan had a personality which shone almost like a beacon-fire in the darkness of the night.

He made both William and Lionel pale into insignificance, and while she was acutely aware of him she felt Sir Roderick was too.

As she had done every night when dinner was over, she left the gentlemen to their port.

Usually they joined her within ten minutes, but she knew as she waited in the Salon that every second seemed a century because she was separated from Vulcan.

All she could do was wonder what he was feeling and if he was thinking of her.

Yesterday he had told her that she had come into his life and he could never let her go. She had known that he had spoken the truth when he said:

"I shall be counting the seconds, my little goddess, until to-morrow evening."

She had counted the seconds all day and now she was not sure of what Vulcan felt about her and if he wanted to hold her in his arms and kiss her as he had done after asking her to go with him to Paris.

Did he still want her? Would he now want to marry her? Was his love deeper than his desire for adventure?

The questions seemed to whirl round her, repeating and re-repeating themselves.

Then she heard the gentlemen's voices as they came from the Dining-Room and felt her heart beating as if it might jump from her breast because in a moment Vulcan would be near her again.

He came into the room walking beside Sir Roderick and talking with an ease that made her feel as if she must run towards him to ask him to put his arms round her and hold her close.

"Love me! Love me!" she willed as he came towards her.

His eyes were, however, not on her face but on the pictures on the walls.

"I see you have a new Van Dyke," he said looking towards one that had been hung in the centre of the wall between the door and the fireplace.

"Do you like it?" Sir Roderick asked.

"I think he is the only artist who could have done you justice, Uncle Roderick."

Sir Roderick smiled, delighted at the compliment.

"I have often thought that myself," he said. "And who would you suggest would be the best artist to paint Astara? Two Italians who tried to capture her on canvas failed utterly."

For the first time since he had entered the room Vulcan looked at Astara.

To her his eyes seemed to flicker over her amost dispassionately.

She looked up at him feeling he must be aware of how much she was loving him and how she wanted him to understand why she had deceived him.

"There are only two people who could do Astara justice," Vulcan said at length, "Botticelli – and myself!"

Astara gasped as he said the last word and Sir Roderick said:

"An excellent idea! When will you paint her?"

"I doubt if you would appreciate the result," Vulcan replied, "but of course like everything else it is a question of time."

"Are we to infer from you that you are going away again?" William asked.

He had come into the room behind his uncle and Astara had not even realised he was there.

"Very shortly," Vulcan replied.

"Then perhaps Astara will have a lucky escape in not having to submit to sitting for you," William said, "especially since, if I may suggest it, you are not well known enough to have the privilege of such a uniquely beautiful model."

There was no doubt that William intended to be unpleasant.

But as if Sir Roderick had no intention of allowing the friction between the two cousins to continue, he merely said to Vulcan:

"Come and look at the pictures I have acquired in these

last two years. You come and show them to him, too, Astara. After all, they are as much your choice as mine."

Astara moved quickly to Sir Roderick's side.

She saw the expression on William's face as she did so and felt inclined to laugh.

For the first time since he had come to Worfield House William's nose was out of joint, and like a spoilt, small boy he was extremely put out and annoyed by the fact.

Sir Roderick showed all his new purchases with an inescapable pride.

They walked round the Salon looking at those already hung. Astara was not surprised to learn how knowledgeable Vulcan was or how with one word or a short sentence he could make her see more clearly than she ever had before the quality of each particular artist.

"A wayward genius!" he said of Piera de Cosimo and she knew no-one could have described his painting better.

"What do you think of this one by Jan Van Eyele?" she asked a little breathlessly.

"His pictures always have a dazzling self-possession and confidence," Vulcan replied.

"And Rubens?" her uncle asked.

Astara waited. She knew how proud Sir Roderick was of the Rubens they had bought in Paris. She felt that if Vulcan disparaged it in any way, it would hurt his uncle.

"Rubens always 'thought' with his brush," Vulcan answered. "He magnified life and glorified it."

Sir Roderick was delighted.

"I have moved my father's sporting pictures to the Library and the Hall," he said as they reached the door of the Salon. "I would like your opinion as to whether a Wootton which he bought just before he died is genuine. I have a feeling that it was done either by one of his pupils or is perhaps a complete fake."

They walked across the Hall towards the Library and Astara realised with relief that William and Lionel had not followed them.

There were only a few candles burning in the Library and Sir Roderick ordered a footman to light the others.

In the big room with its background of books, Astara stood watching Vulcan as he inspected the painting.

She hoped that perhaps he would touch her hand or say something reassuring when Sir Roderick was looking the other way.

He must be aware, she thought, of her feelings. He must know how anxious she was that he should not be angry with her.

But if he did know what she felt, he made no sign of it.

When finally he said good-bye she thought despairingly it would be impossible to go through the night and wait until the morning before she could see him alone.

Sir Roderick saw him off from the Hall, and although she walked beside him Vulcan continued to talk to his uncle.

"I would have liked you to stay here," Sir Roderick was saying, "but I suppose you are very comfortable in the old Mill which I hear you have made charming."

"You must come and see it, Uncle Roderick," Vulcan replied, "though it can hardly compare with the magnificence of Worfield House!"

"There is a great deal more I wish to do now that I am living here," Sir Roderick replied, "and I hope you will help me, at least as far as the pictures are concerned."

"There is nothing I would enjoy more," Vulcan answered, "but I am afraid I am soon off on my travels and have a great deal to do before I go."

"Then try to spare me a little of your valuable time," Sir Roderick said with a slightly cynical accent on the word "valuable".

"I am sure my cousins are far more capable of doing what you want than I am," Vulcan said, and now there was a definite innuendo behind the words.

The two men looked at each other.

"You are quite sure about that?" Sir Roderick asked.

"Quite sure!" Vulcan answered.

He put out his hand.

"Good-night, Uncle Roderick, and thank you for a most interesting dinner."

Astara held her breath. Could he really have meant what he had said?

She would know for certain, she thought, when he touched her. But before she could hold out her hand towards him Vulcan bowed.

"Good-night, Miss Beverley," he said. "It has been delightful to meet you!"

Then he was gone out through the front door and only by exerting every ounce of her will-power did Astara prevent herself from running after him.

"How can you leave me like this?" she wanted to cry. "How can you be so cruel?"

As if in a dream she heard her uncle ask if she wished to retire.

She must have given him the right answer for the next thing she knew she was in her Bed-Room, alone and the tears were streaming down her face.

She had lost everything . . everything which mattered in the whole world!

CHAPTER SIX

Astara hurried through the wood, not actually running but walking as quickly as she possibly could.

It was only seven o'clock but she was sure that Vulcan, like her father, was an early riser.

She was half-afraid that he might already have left and gone perhaps to London before she could see him.

She had been unable to sleep and had lain awake wondering what she should do. But every possible solution seemed hopeless or impracticable and ended in her once again crying hopelessly.

She loved him so overwhelmingly that it was an agony to know that he was, despite all he had said, prepared to give her up and never see her again.

This morning she was not interested in the beauty of the wood or the early morning sunshine percolating through the trees. All she could think of was to reach Little Milden as quickly as possible to find Vulcan.

Perhaps, she tried to tell herself, she had misunderstood what he had said to her uncle.

Yet if she was honest she knew that the way he had virtually ignored her during the evening and deliberately avoided touching her when they said good-night was significant in itself.

She reached the old Mill and for the first time since she had come there she found the door closed.

First she thought frantically that she was too late, Vulcan had gone and she would never see him again.

Then she told herself it was still very early in the morning and perhaps he was not yet up or was at breakfast.

She did not knock on the door, she merely lifted the latch and walked in.

Everything seemed very quiet and she resisted the impulse to call to Vulcan and to learn that, if he answered, he was still in the Mill.

Then she heard a movement in the room where he painted and she walked through the doorway to see him placing his pictures in a packing-case.

She stood still, looking at him while he continued to pack the canvasses neatly side by side in the wooden container as if she was not there.

She knew he was aware of her presence although he gave no sign of it.

At last because she could bear the silence no longer she said:

"I . . I want to talk to . . you, Vulcan."

She was surprised how strange her own voice sounded.

"There is nothing to talk about," he replied without looking up, apparently intent on what he was doing.

"Will you . . listen to me?"

"I will listen, but it is a waste of words."

"But why? Why must you . . behave like . . this?"

"You know the answer to that. You live in one world and I live in another, and nothing we do or say can bridge it."

"That is not . . true."

Astara moved forward as she spoke drawing nearer to him until she stood beside the packing-case.

He picked up another canvas and she asked:

"Are you . . angry with me?"

"No, why should I be? But if you play with fire you are liable to get burnt."

"You thought I was a village maiden and wanted me to pose for your picture."

"If I remember rightly, I thought you were Aphrodite

come from Olympus to help in what to me was a real dilemma."

"I wanted to help you . . I was glad to do so, but now you . . have no . . further . . use for me."

There was so much unhappiness in her tone that almost involuntarily he raised his eyes to look at her for the first time.

She was standing the other side of the packing-case and because the curtains were not drawn over the window the light on her hair made it appear that she was haloed by it.

But her eyes, which seemed to fill her whole face were dark and unhappy and her lips trembled as she said:

"Please . . Vulcan, do not . . leave me."

For a moment it seemed as if he found it impossible to answer her, as if despite every resolution his whole being went out towards her.

Then in a voice that was harsh and over-loud and seemed to echo round the big room, he said:

"For God's sake, do not make it worse! You know as well as I do that we have to part."

"Why? Why?" she asked. "I love you! I am not ashamed to say it . . I love you!"

"You will forget me."

"That will be . . impossible!"

"You are very young. However unhappy you may feel now these things pass and when you are older you will know that I am doing what is right."

"Can it ever be right to refuse love? To turn your back one something so perfect . . so wonderful that I know we . . belong to each other . . or at least . . I belong to you."

There was a note in her voice which seemed to vibrate between them and she thought for a moment that she had broken through his defences, and that he would take her in his arms.

Then he walked away moving towards the North window to stand looking out over the mill-pool and the green fields which bordered the village.

"Go home, Astara," he said, "and think of my uncle's plans for you – the money, the social acclaim and the position you will occupy at Worfield House."

"It could .. be yours."

Astara only whispered the words but he heard them.

"I am not the right man for such a position. You had far better marry one of my cousins and, personally, I should choose Lionel. He is by far the nicer of the two."

Vulcan spoke coldly, but Astara felt that underneath the indifference he forced upon his voice he was suffering in much the same way as she was.

"Do you really imagine that .. loving you as I .. do I would .. marry anyone else?" she asked.

"Of course you will marry!"

Again his voice was loud and over-positive.

"What you feel for me now is the calf-love which every girl experiences with her first love-affair. I can promise you from experience that it is very easy to forget."

"Do you really .. believe that is how I .. feel?" Astara asked. "Do you think that if I were so shallow and so inconsequential I could have portrayed Persephone as you .. wished me to do? It was the love that you .. awoke in me that made you .. see her .. enveloped in .. light."

She had not consciously thought the words but felt that they were there, put into her mind by some power beyond herself.

Vulcan did not answer, he only stood with his back to her, and suddenly through a mist of tears Astara felt as if he had already left her and she was alone.

With a little exclamation that was a cry of pain she ran towards him.

She reached him and inserted herself between him and the window to look up at him, the tears running down her cheeks, her eyes beseeching him as she said:

"I love you! Oh, Vulcan, I love you! I will do .. anything you wish .. you need not .. marry me .. I will come with you to Paris .. or anywhere else in the world. Take me .. please .. take me with .. you!"

Her voice broke on the last words so that they were almost incoherent, and now as if he could no longer resist her Vulcan pulled her into his arms and his mouth came down on hers.

He kissed her fiercely, almost brutally, first her lips, then her eyes, the tears from her cheeks, and again her lips.

It was as if a tempest swept over her, and yet she was not afraid. She only knew his mouth evoked the same wonder and glory within her as he had done before.

She felt as if her whole body was invaded with the light he had painted in his picture, but now it was no longer clear and cold but burning as if it came from the very heart of the sun.

He kissed her until she could think of nothing but the wonder of him and a rapture which seemed to grow in intensity within herself.

She only knew she was his and he was hers.

He picked her up in his arms, still holding her lips captive. Her eyes were shut but she felt him carrying her across the room.

"I love you! Oh, Vulcan, I love you!" she wanted to cry, but everything was too glorious, too perfect for speech and her whole body was burning with the flames of love.

Then suddenly, so suddenly that she could hardly realise what was happening, Vulcan set her down on her feet.

"Go home and forget me," he said, "and God knows, I shall try to forget you."

Astara could not realise what was happening or where she was!

The suddenness of Vulcan's movement had left her unsteady so that she put out her hand and found she was holding onto the side of the door.

It was the front door of the Mill.

She heard it close behind her, heard the key turn in the lock. Then there were Vulcan's footsteps moving heavily along the flagged passage.

She was outside, alone in the sunshine which had no warmth in it.

. . . .

Somehow, she could never afterwards remember anything about it, Astara walked back to Worfield House.

By the time she reached it she felt as if her whole body had gone numb and there was a darkness in her mind which made it almost impossible to think.

She must have gone upstairs, because a little while later she came down again to the Breakfast-Room.

It was as if her body acted instinctively without her will, without her conscious volition.

She could no longer think, she was past tears.

"Good-morning, Astara!" Sir Roderick said.

She kissed his cheek as she always did and took her place opposite him at the end of the table.

William and Lionel who had risen as she entered resumed their seats and continued their breakfast.

The servants poured out her coffee and she refused several dishes that were offered to her.

"We shall not be able to ride until about half-past ten," Sir Roderick said. "It is annoying, but I have to see these men from the Council."

"They are usually very long-winded," Lionel remarked sympathetically.

"Not with me," Sir Roderick replied.

"I have an idea that while we are waiting for Uncle Roderick," William said addressing Astara, "you might like to try out my new team of bays."

Astara did not answer and he went on:

"I will drive them for a short while to take the freshness out of them, then if you wish you can drive them home. I know you will appreciate how easy they are to handle."

Vaguely at the back of her mind Astara remembered that she had always wanted to drive a team of four, but now it seemed unimportant whether she did or not.

"Shall we do that?" William asked.

She knew he would be astonished if she refused such an offer.

"Y . yes . . yes, of course," she replied.

"I will order them for nine-thirty," he said.

Then he looked across the table at Lionel and said:

"I regret that my Phaeton will not hold more than two people."

"I am aware of that," Lionel answered.

William smiled as if he thought he had scored a point over his cousin in ensuring that he had Astara to himself.

Sir Roderick rose from the end of the table.

"I imagine the Councillors will be waiting for me," he said, "but I assure you I shall be back at the house by half after ten."

"We will be ready, Uncle Roderick," Lionel replied.

As if Sir Roderick's departure made Astara realise that she too could leave the Breakfast-Room she rose.

Lionel opened the door for her and followed her into the passage.

"Do not let William monopolise you for too long," he said. "He is taking an unfair advantage in offering to let you drive his Phaeton. I could hardly invite you to share the saddle of my charger if I had him with me!"

Astara tried to smile at his joke but it was a pitiful effort.

She wondered if she should refuse to go with William and instead lock herself in her Bed-Room.

Then she told herself that tears would not help her nor would anything else.

Vulcan had meant what he said and somehow her life must go on, even though she felt as if she was crippled and maimed in a way that no-one except he would understand.

He must have known, she thought, that by sending her away, by refusing the love she offered him, he had struck a mortal blow not at her body but at her very soul.

Only Vulcan knew that their love was not only physical but spiritual, and without him everything he had aroused in her would wither away and die so that she could only be a ghost of herself.

"How can he do this to me?" she asked.

Then her education, her training, the self-control that her father and mother had taught her to exert ever since she was a child, forced her to behave in what an uninformed on-looker would have thought a normal manner.

She told her maid what bonnet she required and which of her expensive silk shawls she would take with her in case it was cold in the Phaeton.

Now that the sun had risen fully it was obvious it would be a hot day, and Astara did not change from the thin white gown she had put on first thing.

She had chosen it deliberately because it was like the one in which she had posed for Vulcan as Persephone, and instinctively she had thought she would remind him that he had called her "Aphrodite" and "his little goddess".

Her white gown was unrelieved by colour but her bonnet was trimmed with a wreath of small pink roses and there were pink ribbons to match, to tie under her chin.

She looked very lovely as she came down the stairs to where William was waiting for her in the Hall.

Only someone more perceptive than he would have realised that she was very pale and her eyes had a glazed look as if she was suffering from shock.

The Phaeton was waiting outside the door. William's exceptionally fine team of bays were fidgeting to be off and the grooms were finding it hard to hold them.

Lionel helped Astara up into the Phaeton.

"Take care of yourself," he said. "These vehicles can be dangerous in narrow country lanes."

"Are you casting aspersions on my driving?" William asked truculently.

"I think I am more apprehensive in case Astara is not as experienced as you," Lionel replied.

William did not answer and he went on:

"Personally I think, whatever you may say about your

horses, they are too head-strong for a woman to control."

"I think you can trust to my judgement," William said loftily, "and Uncle Roderick assures me that Astara is a most proficient driver!"

Lionel reached up to touch Astara's hand.

"I am prepared to believe that you are proficient at everything!" he said. "At the same time I shall be waiting anxiously for your return."

William made a sound that might have been an expression of irritation or disgust and signalled to the grooms to release the horses' heads.

He cracked his whip and Lionel was forced to step back, but he stood watching Astara and William until they were out of sight amongst the great oak trees in the Park.

Then with a sigh he walked towards the stables.

. . . .

Astara found it impossible to feel anything but a great aching void within herself.

She should have been delighted to be sitting beside such an excellent driver and behind such outstanding horseflesh.

Her knowledge of horses made her aware that the bays, all perfectly matched, their only markings being two white fetlocks, were a team that one might be able to purchase only once in a lifetime.

William's Phaeton too was more lightly sprung and certainly smarter in appearance than anything she had seen in Paris.

With his top-hat on the side of his handsome head he certainly embellished the whole turn-out in a manner, she thought, that one would only find in England.

Despite Lionel's warnings they moved at a sharp pace along the hedge-bordered lanes in which, as she had noticed on her way down from London, there were primroses, violets and other spring flowers that she had not seen for many years.

There were golden kingcups by the side of the streams and there was a fragrance in the air.

But for her there was only the barren cold of winter within her heart, and it would be impossible ever again to thrill to the miracle of the spring because it would remind her of Vulcan's picture of Persephone.

"How can you do this to me? How can you make me suffer like this?" she cried and thought that her misery must wing its way back to him!

Surely he must be aware of how deeply and cruelly he was hurting her?

Intent on his driving William did not speak, and immersed in her unhappiness Astara ceased to think of the horses, the country through which they were passing or of anything except Vulcan.

She could still feel the pressure of his lips on hers, in fact her mouth was slightly bruised by his violence, and yet she was aware that something wild and primitive within herself had responded to it.

She had known instinctively, she thought, from the first moment she saw Vulcan that he was the man who complemented her femininity by his masculinity.

He was her mate, the other half of her soul, the man who perhaps had been her lover in past incarnations, whom she had always sought and now had found again.

And she was sure he felt the same even while he would not acknowledge it.

There had been a fusion between them from the first moment they had looked into each other's eyes, and when he kissed her she had known that he had awakened her soul and made it his.

"How can he deny all that," she asked, "and for what? His exploration of the world, the penetration of places where other men dare not go, the discovery of forgotten civilisations? Could that really be more important than love?"

The answer was conclusive – to Vulcan it was.

She felt as if he had thrown her from the Heaven into

which her love for him had taken her into the deepest and darkest hell, far worse than any Hades in which Persephone had been incarcerated.

It was not only losing him, it was losing love and the hope of any chance of happiness.

Astara might be young, but she had thought very deeply. Perhaps as her mother and father believed, she was an "old soul" retaining instinctively the knowledge and growth of mind which were the product of other lives.

She knew now that as far as she was concerned the life she had to live in her present body would always be incomplete and without depth.

She would go on breathing and growing older, but everything that mattered, everything that was of importance, had ceased from this moment because Vulcan was no longer with her.

She came back to reality with a start to hear William say:

"I thought you would think this part of the countryside rather attractive, which is why I brought you here."

Astara looked around.

As he said it was attractive, thickly wooded but with occasional glimpses of fields and of fruit-trees coming into blossom.

"What is the time?" she asked. "We must not keep Uncle Roderick waiting."

"If he does wait for us I am afraid it will be in vain," William replied.

"What do you mean?" Astara asked. "You know he dislikes our not being ready when he is and he looks forward to our rides."

"This morning he will have to make do with just Lionel as a companion," William replied. "You and I are playing truant."

"I do not understand."

"We are having luncheon at a special place which I know will interest you."

"Did you tell Uncle Roderick so before we left?"

"I left a note for him on his desk."

"I hope he finds it before he waits for us," Astara said, "Why did you not give it to a servant?"

William did not reply and she thought it was extremely tiresome of him to interfere with Sir Roderick's arrangements.

Like all elderly men who organise their lives down to the last detail it infuriated him to have any of his plans changed at the last moment.

He had said he would be back by ten-thirty and Astara knew that he would be back at the house a few minutes before and would expect her and his two nephews to be waiting for him.

"We must turn back," she said. "I am sure if you apologise Uncle Roderick will forgive you for being inconsiderate, and if he has started on his ride without us we can catch him up."

"For once Uncle Roderick is not going to have his own way," William said in what she thought was an aggressive tone. "I find it difficult, Astara, ever to get you to myself and therefore I have planned what we will do to-day very carefully."

"I wish you had consulted me first."

"If I had you might have refused to come with me."

"I should certainly have insisted that we were back by the time Uncle Roderick expected us."

"Then you see how wise I was not to risk an argument which inevitably I should have won."

"How can you be sure of that?"

"I always win," William said complacently.

She thought as she had thought before that he was intolerably conceited.

She told herself that perhaps when Sir Roderick realised the high-handed way William had behaved he would not be so obsessed with his favourite nephew.

Then she remembered how delighted Sir Roderick had been to see Vulcan the previous evening.

She could still remember her surprise when he had seemed to know everything that Vulcan had done and had been, she was sure, proud of his courage and daring in reaching Mecca and Harrar.

The mere thought of Vulcan brought back the agony within her breast and she told herself sharply that she would not think of him.

"Where are we going?" she asked William. "And how soon will we be there?"

"I am taking you to luncheon at '*The Kind Dragon*'," he answered. "It is an Inn built on a lake near a village called Elstree. In the summer I often drive out there in the evenings for dinner."

Astara realised that William was determined to take her to "*The Kind Dragon*" and there seemed to be no point in arguing any further. She therefore relapsed into silence until about thirty minutes later when William exclaimed:

"Here is the lake. Now you will see that I have not exaggerated its attractions."

They had turned off the main highway, and were making their way along a narrow road bordered by trees which ran beside a long lake, which appeared to be in the centre of a forest.

The sun was shining on it and there were a number of wild ducks and other birds which rose at their approach.

The road extended along one side of the lake until at the far end Astara could see an ancient Inn with a sloping roof built on the very edge of the water.

"There is '*The Kind Dragon*'!" William said pointing with his whip.

"It is certainly very picturesque," Astara replied.

She thought it was very high-handed of him to have brought her here without asking her first if it was something she wished to do.

But she realised that while she had been thinking of Vulcan they had driven far further than she had expected and now it was too late to return in time for luncheon.

She could only hope that William had given Sir Roderick a plausible explanation in the note he had left on his desk.

They drew up outside the Inn which was very old and painted black and white which reminded Astara of the way that Vulcan had painted the Mill.

The ostlers ran to the horses' heads as William alighted first from the Phaeton to help Astara to the ground.

"I expect you would like to wash and tidy yourself before luncheon," he said. "I will order a Bed-Room for you and as we have a private parlour to ourselves you can take off your bonnet and be comfortable."

"Thank you," Astara murmured.

She walked up a narrow oak staircase and a mob-capped Chambermaid showed her into an attractive room with a bow window that overlooked the lake.

Astara stood for a moment staring at the sunshine on the water.

Irrepressibly it came to her mind that if she were here with Vulcan everything would vibrate with happiness.

Instead she could only tell herself she must behave sensibly so that William would not realise that anything was wrong.

She could not bear him to know how she was suffering or that Vulcan had come into her life and left it a barren desert.

She had heard the way he spoke to his cousin last night and she had seen what she thought was a look of contempt in his eyes.

She knew it would be impossible for William ever to understand that Vulcan's standards and ideals were very different from his.

With a start she realised she had been staring out of the window at the lake and had made no effort to get ready for luncheon.

She took off her bonnet, looked at herself in the mirror and wondered why her face was not lined with suffering and changed beyond recognition.

The maid had poured some hot water into a china basin and she washed her hands, then walked down the stairs.

The Landlord was waiting at the foot of them and led her down a narrow heavily beamed passage to open the door at the end of it.

The private parlour was small, panelled with ancient oak, and the table for luncheon was set beside a window through which Astara could see a well-tended garden.

"I hope you are hungry," William said. "I have ordered what I am sure you will find a delicious meal."

Astara thought it would be impossible for her to force even a mouthful of food down her throat, but aloud she said:

"This seems a very luxurious place to be out in the wilds."

"I told you that I come here sometimes in the summer," William said, "and it is in the Season a fashionable haunt of the Bucks of St. James's."

Astara suspected that the women they brought to "*The Kind Dragon*" were of a different status from herself, and she thought that in a way William was being insulting in bringing her here unchaperoned.

But there was no point in saying so and as the Landlord came bustling in with their luncheon she sat down at the table.

The food was excellent and William was apparently satisfied with the wine.

Astara ate very little, but he did full justice to the many courses and she had the feeling that he was deliberately prolonging the meal.

When at last he sat back in his chair with a glass of brandy in his hand and the servants withdrew from the room Astara said:

"We must be getting back. I am sure already Uncle Roderick will be very annoyed with us."

William put his glass of brandy down on the table before he said:

"We are not going back!"

Astara thought she could not have heard him correctly.
"What did you say?" she asked.
"I said we are not going back – not until to-morrow, at any rate."
"W . what . . are you . . saying?"
"This may come as somewhat of a surprise to you, Astara," William replied, "but we are being married in an hour's time!"
Astara stared at him across the table.
"Are you mad?"
"On the contrary, I am extremely sane," he replied. "You have played with me quite long enough, Astara, and as apparently you cannot make up your own mind I am making it up for you!"
"If you really think I am willing to marry you, you are very much mistaken!" Astara cried.
"You have no choice in the matter!"
She drew in her breath, but her voice was quite steady as she asked:
"What do you . . mean by that?"
"I sent my Valet to London at dawn this morning," William replied, "to procure a Special Licence. He should be here by now, and I have already sent a groom to arrange with the Parson whose Church is within half-a-mile of this Inn, to marry us."
"Let me make this quite clear," Astara said quietly. "I have no intention of marrying you."
"As I have already told you," William replied, "you have no choice."
"Do you intend to drag me screaming up the aisle? I imagine no Parson would perform a Service when the bride categorically says no!"
"If that is your intention this afternoon, then the marriage will be postponed until tomorrow morning!"
There was something in the way he spoke that made Astara, for the first time, feel afraid.
She was alone with a man in an isolated Inn.
She had seen from the way he was greeted on his arrival

and from the way the Inn-keeper had spoken to him during the meal, that he was a frequent visitor to the Inn and was considered a person of importance.

This meant, Astara knew, that if she appealed to the Inn-keeper or the other servants to help her they would not be prepared to do so.

She also thought quickly that if William forced her to stay the night in the Inn with him she would have no alternative the following morning but to become his wife.

She could not help feeling that the way he was forcing her into this position would not really shock or horrify his uncle or anyone except perhaps Lionel.

They would consider it was a sensible, advantageous marriage from both hers and William's point of view.

It was, after all, what Sir Roderick desired.

She thought as she had thought before that he had merely included his other two nephews in his arrangements simply to make the whole idea seem more attractive to her.

It was William whom Sir Roderick had chosen to inherit Worfield House, and how he coerced her into marriage would not ultimately be of any consequence.

She wanted to scream, she wanted to run from the room and away from the Inn, but she knew that William would not let her escape. Any attempt to do so would be merely humiliating.

"I suppose it does not matter to you," she said aloud, her voice icy and yet restrained, "that I am in love with somebody else?"

"Vulcan, I suppose!" William answered. "I saw the way you looked at him last night. It made me realise he was dangerous."

He laughed and it was an unpleasant sound.

"Women are always fascinated by wasters and vagabonds, and you are no exception."

"That is an unfair criticism!" Astara replied hotly.

"Unfair or not," William retorted, "I have no intention of allowing my uncle's wealth and the family estate to be wasted on a ne'er-do-well like my Cousin Vulcan."

"You are behaving abominably!" Astara stormed. "Let me make this quite clear . . I hate you! I would rather die than marry you!"

William laughed again.

"You will not die, my dear, and I can assure you that you will enjoy being married to me. As I have already said, I can bring you every social advantage and you will find that money compensates for a great many other deficiencies."

"All the money in the world would not compensate me for having you as my husband!" Astara retorted.

"You think that now," William replied, "but you will grow to love me, perhaps regrettably quickly. I find your defiance intriguing and rather exciting."

There was a look in his eyes that made Astara shrink within herself.

She knew that he spoke the truth and that, because she was not as complaisant as his other women had been, she excited him.

He not only wanted the money that the marriage would bring him but herself.

He wanted her in a way she knew was not love, but something she had never encountered before and was called lust.

She rose from the table and realised as she did so that William was watching her warily as if he thought she might be inclined to make a bolt for it.

She stood in front of the fireplace in which one large log was smouldering.

Astara was aware that she felt very cold and she knew it was shock and because she was also afraid.

Now over and over in her mind like an animal caught in a trap, she was trying to think of a way of escape; something she could do, something she could say that would prevent William from marrying her as he intended to do.

She was wondering which would be worse, to marry him this afternoon or to wait until the following morning.

She was quite certain that if she played for time and was kept a prisoner in the Inn, she would not, however hard she fought, be able to prevent him from making her his.

She might plead with him, she might beg him to spare her, but she had seen the glint in his eyes when he looked at her and she knew he would show her no mercy and there would in fact be no escape.

William rose from the table to come and stand beside her:

"I can see you intend to be sensible about this," he said. "Scenes would get us nowhere and in case you are unaware of it the Landlord will agree to anything I suggest and there are in fact no other guests in the Inn."

"I loathe you!" Astara said in a low voice. "You are everything that is foul and despicable!"

William smiled.

"As I have already told you, you will change your mind and by to-morrow morning you will be thanking God on your knees that you have such an exceptional man as your husband!"

She knew by the way he spoke that he thought she would find him such an admirable lover, as other women had done in the past, that her opposition and indignation would fade away in the night.

The very thought of being touched by William when she loved Vulcan made her shiver.

She looked up at him and wondered how she had ever thought for a moment that he was attractive or that there was anything to commend him.

Now she knew that she would rather embrace a serpent and that she had spoken the truth when she had said she would rather die than become his wife.

Then some part of her brain swept away her fear and the last vestige of the numbness which had made her find it difficult to think ever since she had left Vulcan.

She began to consider without emotion what she should do.

She knew that William was standing watching her and she thought that what made it more unpleasant than anything else was that he was so self-assured, so absolutely confident that he had won.

She remembered Lionel saying that William must always be first, always be the winner, and that was what he meant to be now.

"I suppose there is no point in making one last appeal to your better nature," Astara asked aloud, "and to your sense of . . decency?"

"Not the slightest!"

"You realise that Uncle Roderick will be very disappointed not to be present at our marriage?"

"I wondered when you would use that argument," he said cynically. "It is no use, Astara. I have made my plans and I do not propose to deviate from them."

He waited, and as she did not speak he went on:

"The only choice you have is whether you marry me to-day or to-morrow morning."

"As I am conventional I prefer that this farce of the Sacred Ceremony should take place now!" Astara said sharply.

She looked around the parlour.

"I assume you will permit me to put on my bonnet? It is usual to wear one in Church."

"Of course!" William said, "but I shall be waiting for you at the bottom of the stairs, and there is no other way by which you can leave the Inn."

"Thank you for saving me the trouble of looking for one," Astara answered sarcastically.

She walked towards the door, William opened it for her and she passed him with her head held high.

She thought there was a smile of amusement on his lips and longed to strike him in the face and to rage and scream at him, but she knew it would do no good.

For the moment he was the master, the conqueror and she was as helpless as any slave.

She went to the Bed-Room she had used before and as

she shut the door she was not surprised to find that there was no key in the lock and no bolt.

It was what she might have expected.

The sight of the large double bed made her shudder and after one glance she walked past it towards the window wondering frantically what she could do.

She imagined that William would give her about five, perhaps ten minutes to prepare herself, before he came upstairs to fetch her and take her forcibly, if necessary, to the Church.

She stood at the window looking out onto the sunlit water and thinking that this could not be happening to her.

A week ago perhaps it would not have seemed so horrifying, but now she had met Vulcan and she knew that William had spoken the truth when he said the expression in her eyes when she looked at Vulcan made him aware of the danger of losing her.

He was not to know she had already lost Vulcan, but that was beside the point.

She still loved him, loved him so that the mere idea of any other man touching her was a sacrilege and an offence against everything she knew to be divine.

"Papa, help me! You have been in dangerous, difficult situations in the past and you have always escaped from them. Tell me now what I must do. Help me . . help me!"

It was a cry that came from the very depths of her being. Then as she opened her eyes she knew that the answer came as if it had been spoken aloud.

She took off her shoes and as if to reassure herself of its width, she picked up the hem of her skirt.

Fortunately the fashion in gowns made them no longer so straight and narrow as they had been during the years of the war and immediately afterwards.

Skirts were now wide at the bottom narrowing to a high waist, with a bodice elaborately trimmed with lace or embroidery.

Without wasting any more time Astara opened wide the casement window and began to climb out.

She looked down at the water of the lake immediately below her as she did so, and estimated that it was deep enough for her to dive and not hit the bottom.

It would be extremely ignominious and it might also be dangerous to be stuck in the mud or to hit her head on the stones. But the Inn was not a high building and Astara reckoned that the lake was not much over twenty feet below her.

She raised herself, holding onto the casement, then dived downwards with the grace of a swallow!

The water was cold and Astara gasped as she came to the surface, then she began to swim with strong rhythmic strokes away from the Inn.

She decided that her best course of action would be to make for the end of the lake and move through the shelter of the woods until she reached the main road.

Then perhaps she could find someone to take pity on her and agree to carry her back towards Worfield House.

She had, however, swum only a little way when she heard a shout behind her and looked back.

She knew before she turned what she would see.

The sound came from William who was leaning out of the Bed-Room window.

"Come back, Astara! Come back!" he ordered.

She turned her head away and went on swimming.

He had discovered her escape sooner than she had expected; perhaps he had been afraid that she would find some way to evade him the moment she was out of his sight.

She swam on finding herself slightly hampered by her skirt, at the same time knowing that if she could reach the shelter of the trees on the far shore before William caught up with her, she had a good chance of escape.

Then, to her consternation, when the end of the lake was still some way away she heard the sound of horse's hoofs and saw him galloping on horse-back along the road by which they had approached the Inn.

She guessed he had borrowed a mount from somebody

who had called at the Inn, or else one of his own horses had been saddled in double-quick time.

However he had done it he was in fact riding along the lake-side, and she knew now that he could reach the end of it as quickly as she could and would intercept her as she stepped from the water.

She ceased swimming except to keep herself afloat.

Perhaps the best thing, she thought, would be to make for the opposite shore. There was no roadway there and it would take William time to ride round the end and he would have to move slowly between the trees.

But then she would be a long way from the main road and isolated from any help.

"What shall I do?" she asked herself.

Then she felt her heart leap.

Coming from the end of the lake where it joined the country lane were two riders and even as she glanced at them Astara knew who they were.

She turned and started to swim rapidly towards the road, and as she did so she saw that watching her William had drawn in the horse he was riding and was at a standstill.

She felt that he must be puzzled as to why she was moving directly towards him until a moment later she saw him turn his head towards the approaching horsemen.

He must have recognised them as she had done and she could guess without seeing him closely the anger on his face.

. . . .

Vulcan and Lionel without checking their pace reached William and drew in their horses sharply.

"What the devil are you doing here?" William asked furiously.

The words seemed almost to hiss from between his lips.

"That is what we have come to ask you," Lionel replied.

Vulcan, without speaking had flung himself from his horse. Instinctively as if he had asked him to do so Lionel bent forward to take the bridle.

"Get down, William!" Vulcan commanded. "I am going to teach you a lesson which has been long overdue!"

"Do you really imagine you can do that?" William asked.

There was no doubt of the sneer in his tone and in the twist of his lips.

"Get down!" Vulcan said again ominously.

William swung himself to the ground.

The horse he had been riding was a quiet one and merely put his head down and started to crop the grass beside the lake.

"If you wish to fight me, Vulcan," he said, "I am quite prepared for you to do so, provided you agree that when I am the winner, which I shall undoubtedly be, you go home, mind your own business and leave Astara to me."

"I will make no bargains with you," Vulgan replied.

He moved towards him.

"Wait a moment," William said. "If we must fight we fight in a sportsman-like and civilised manner. I wish to take off my coat."

As he spoke he pulled off his elegant, tight-fitting whipcord riding-jacket, and put it down on the ground.

Then swiftly so that it might have been considered a foul he struck out at Vulcan.

Lionel seeing William's action drew in his breath, but Vulcan side-stepped the blow and hit back.

He punched him and now it was William who drew back with his fists on guard.

"Keep to the rules," he said sharply.

"I learnt in a different school from you," Vulcan replied.

He went at William again and the acclaimed pugilist, the boxing Viscount who had boasted that he had sparred with Jackson and Mendoza and had defeated them both, went down with a thud.

It might not have been in the Queensberry Rules, Lionel decided, but Vulcan had used very effectively a type of action that he had never seen before.

Whatever the method William was out for the count and Vulcan picked him up as if he was a sack of coals and tossed him into the water.

As he did so he saw about two of three yards away Astara reach the side of the lake.

She stood up, her soaked gown revealing every curve of her young body and making her appear like a nymph or one of the Sirens who had enticed Ulysses.

She would have walked the last few steps towards the bank, but Vulcan was there before her.

He walked into the lake, pulled her close against him and bent his head to kiss her cold lips.

CHAPTER SEVEN

Somebody came into the parlour and without turning his head Vulcan, who was standing by the window, asked:

"How is the young lady?"

"See for yourself!" a voice replied.

He swung round and saw Astara smiling at him from the other end of the room.

She was wearing a gingham gown belonging to one of the chambermaids, there was a towel round her shoulders and her golden hair fell over it in heavy waves.

"You are all right?"

Vulcan's voice was surprisingly hoarse.

"I thought I would .. finish drying my .. hair in .. front of the .. fire," she answered.

Her eyes were on his but she spoke as if the words she were saying did not really come from her brain.

She was thinking of the rapture he brought her when she stepped from the lake into his arms and he had kissed her so that she forgot everything but the wonder of being close to him again.

Then he had put her down on the bank of the lake, pulled off his coat, put it round her shoulders and lifting her had set her on the saddle of his horse.

He mounted behind her and only when he was holding her close against him did he turn his head to say to Lionel:

"Follow us to the Inn. You had better leave that swine a horse to carry him."

"I am afraid he might drown," Lionel said looking to where William seemed to be floating on the water.

"It is what he deserves," Vulcan replied and rode off.

He saw, however, as he spoke that William had obviously recovered consciousness and was threshing the water with his hands.

Vulcan had not spoken as he rode at some speed back towards the Inn, and because she was so thankful he had saved her and so thrilled to be in his arms, Astara merely put her head against his shoulder and shut her eyes.

Then a few minutes later she murmured:

"I am .. making you .. wet."

"It does not matter," Vulcan answered.

They reached the yard of the Inn and as an ostler ran to the head of the horse Vulcan leapt to the ground, then lifted Astara very carefully from the saddle.

"Show me which is this lady's room!"

As if he recognised the tone of authority the Landlord ran ahead up the oak staircase and opened the door of the Bed-Room.

"Send two Chambermaids here!" Vulcan ordered.

"Yes, M'Lord, immediately, M'Lord!" the Inn-keeper replied obsequiously.

Almost before he had finished speaking his wife and a Chambermaid hurried into the Bed-Room.

They helped Astara out of her wet clothes and dried her hair, but all the time she was impatient to hurry downstairs and find Vulcan.

Now she thought there was an expression in his eyes that she had never seen before and she was not certain what it could mean.

She wanted to go close to him, to hold onto him and beg him once again not to leave her.

Yet because she felt shy she looked towards the fire and said:

"Perhaps I had .. better sit on the .. floor."

Without waiting for an answer she sat down on the hearth-rug with her back to the smouldering logs and Vulcan took some smaller ones from the basket and put them on the fire.

Then he sat down on a chair beside her.

"Are you really all right?" he asked.

He spoke as if he was astonished by her appearance and that she was not swooning or half-unconscious from the ordeal she had been through.

"Of course I am," Astara replied. "I felt quite warm when I was swimming, although the water was cold."

"I had no idea you could swim like that," Vulcan said. "Why did you go into the lake?"

"It was my only way of escape,"' Astara answered. "William intended me to marry him immediately, and as he was waiting at the bottom of the stairs I had to dive from the Bed-Room window-sill."

"Good God!"

It was obvious that Vulcan was surprised.

"I have swum in worse places," Astara said with a smile. "At least there were no crocodiles."

"Crocodiles?" he repeated in a wondering tone. Then he exclaimed:

"Beverley! You are not telling me that you are Charles Beverley's daughter?"

"Of couse I am!" Astara answered. "Did you not know?"

"I had no idea," he replied. "All I heard about you was that Uncle Roderick was giving very large and expensive parties for a young girl in Paris."

He stopped speaking to stare at her almost as if he could not believe his eyes.

"Charles Beverley's daughter! I never suspected – I never dreamt! Then you are the child who went with him to Siam and across the Libyan desert."

Astara laughed.

"I do not remember much about that," she said, "except that I used to sleep with great comfort on the back of a camel and the movement rocked me to sleep."

She saw the expression on Vulcan's face and she said:

"I loved travelling with Papa and these last years since he died I have missed not only being with him, but all the thrilling, exciting, adventurous things we did together."

She gave a little sigh before she went on:

"That is why I wanted to read your book. I knew it would remind me of the articles Papa used to write for the Association in London, and one of the founders of the *Société de Géographes* in Paris told me when I was there that he loved listening to Papa's lectures."

"I heard two of them in which he mentioned you," Vulcan said.

"I remember those," Astara smiled. "I spent hours copying them out so that they were legible."

"How can you have been on all those dangerous and exhausting journeys and yet look as if a puff of wind would blow you away?"

"I am very much tougher than you think."

"And extremely resourceful!"

She looked up at him and for a moment there was silence. Then he said:

"I was thinking before you came into the room that I should have to give up the trip I had planned to the Caucasus. I had promised to bring back a report which the *Société de Géographes* wants particularly."

Astara was very still.

"And . . now?" she asked.

She could hardly breathe the words.

"I will fulfil my obligation," Vulcan replied, "and take you with me."

Astara gave a little cry, then before he could move she was on her knees reaching her arms up towards him.

"Do you . . mean that? Do you really . . mean it?"

He looked down at her with a tenderness that she had never seen in his face before.

"I could hardly leave you behind to be kidnapped and forced into marriage with somebody like my cousin."

"He was . . jealous of the way I . . looked at you."

"So he cheated, as he has done all his life," Vulcan said harshly. "But it is something he will never do again where you are concerned. You belong to me, Astara, and I was mad to think I could live without you."

"You .. thought I would be an .. encumbrance and a .. restriction," Astara murmured.

"I thought apart from the feelings we had for each other we had nothing in common," Vulcan answered.

He put his hands on each side of her face as he went on:

"You will have to forgive me, my darling, but how was I to guess that in spite of your beauty, which makes you like a goddess, and the luxury with which you are surrounded, you were Charles Beverley's daughter and used to a very different sort of life?"

"I thought once that .. it would not matter .. if we were in a .. tent in the desert .. or a cave in the mountains .. as long as .. we were .. together."

"I know that now, and I was a fool," Vulcan said.

He took her in his arms and lifted her onto his knees. Then he was kissing her passionately and demandingly so that she thrilled with the ecstasy his lips always evoked in her.

Now it was more wonderful, more perfect, because she knew she need no longer be afraid of losing him.

When finally he raised his head he looked down at her to say:

"My own precious little Aphrodite, how could I really have contemplated losing you?"

"You will .. never do that," Astara answered, "and I will be .. with you and look after you as Mama looked after Papa."

Vulcan smiled.

"I thought I was going to look after you!"

Astara laughed.

"Mama said men always think that, but really Papa would have forgotten his way, his compass, his maps, and even food, if we had not been there."

"I can see you have been well trained as an explorer's wife!"

She looked up at him with a serious expression on her face.

"Y . you . . need not . . marry me . . if you do not . . want to."

"And always be afraid of losing you? You will marry me immediately! We are due in Paris in four days' time."

"Oh . . Vulcan . . .!"

It was a cry of sheer delight, then as he kissed her holding her close against him, she could feel his heart beating against hers.

His kisses became more demanding, more passionate and she stirred beneath the touch of his hand.

"Do I excite you?" he asked.

"You . . know you . . do. I love you . . . Oh Vulcan . . I love you!"

"Not as much as I want you to love me."

"Then . . teach . . me."

"That is what I intend to do my precious, my adorable little goddess."

There was a deep note in Vulcan's voice and a fire in his eyes which thrilled her wildly.

She threw back her head to look up at him.

"This is . . true? I am not . . dreaming?"

"No, my sweet love – this is real."

"I am so . . happy . . so crazily, unbelievably happy after being so miserable."

"Forgive me."

Vulcan kissed her eyes, then he moved his lips sensuously over the softness of her cheeks, so that she quivered.

As if she aroused him, he lifted her a little higher in his arms and kissed her neck until the breath came quickly through her parted lips.

"I . . love . . you . . . I . . love . . you."

It was difficult to say the words.

The door opened and Lionel came into the room.

Vulcan looked up but he made no attempt to release Astara and she hid her blushes against his shoulder.

"What have you done with that swine?" he enquired.

"He is having to stay in bed until his clothes are dry," Lionel replied.

"You told him we intend to take his Phaeton?"

"I did, and said you would leave him your horse."

"He did not object?"

"He swore at me with a fluency which would have been envied in the Sergeant's Mess, but there was nothing he could do."

"No, nothing!" Vulcan said firmly, "And the sooner we get back to Uncle Roderick the better!"

"Uncle Roderick!" Astara exclaimed as if she had just remembered his existence. "How did you know where to find me?"

"You have Lionel to thank for that," Vulcan answered.

"Tell me," Astara begged.

"It was really just luck," Lionel replied.

He was looking at her in Vulcan's arms and she saw the pain in his eyes. He walked across the room and poured himself a glass of wine from a decanter which stood on the table.

"When you and William drove off," he said after he had taken a sip from the glass, "I walked towards the stables thinking as I had nothing to do I would inspect the horses. Sam was there and I remarked to him what a very fine fine team of bays William had.

" 'They be th' best-matched ones Oi've seen for many a year, Cap'n!' Sam replied. 'But they be over fresh not havin' been out for a day or so an' Oi 'opes 'is Lordship'll drive careful-like.'

" 'That is exactly what I told him,' I remarked.

" 'Well, a long drive's wot they needs,' Sam said.

" 'A long drive?' I exclaimed. 'But His Lordship and Miss Beverley have to be back here in an hour to ride with Sir Roderick.'

"Sam looked surprised.

"''is Lordship tells Oi he'd not be back 'til to-morrow.'

"'Are you certain?' I asked.

"'Quite certain, Cap'n!' Sam answered.

"I was astonished and dismayed," Lionel said, "and walked into the house wondering what to do. It was then I remembered that before you came downstairs I had seen William going into the Library with something in his hand."

He took another sip of wine and continued:

"I thought it was a note. I went into the Library and found what he had carried lying on Uncle Roderick's desk. I had no compunction about opening it."

"That was sensible of you, Lionel," Vulcan remarked.

"I really did not stop to think," Lionel replied. "I just had a feeling that William was up to one of his tricks."

"What did he say in the note?" Astara enquired.

"He said that he had decided to take matters into his own hands and that when he brought you back you would be his wife, and he felt sure it would meet with Uncle Roderick's approval."

"I have an .. uncomfortable feeling that Uncle Roderick might have been pleased," Astara said in a low voice.

"I doubt it," Vulcan replied. "I do not believe that he has ever cared for sneaks and cheats."

"That is exactly what William was doing," Lionel said. "He always cheated at Eton when he wanted to get a prize."

"So what did you do after you read the note?" Astara asked.

"I went back to the stables," Lionel answered, "and told Sam to saddle a horse for me and one for himself and we went to Little Milden."

"To find .. Vulcan?"

"I knew I could not cope with William alone. He had always been able to beat me at everything. If I tried to fight him I knew he would knock me out in a few seconds."

Lionel finished his wine then exclaimed with the enthusiasm of a school-boy:

"How on earth did you do it, Vulcan? I have never seen anything so quick or so neat. God, I wish I could fight like that!"

"As William said, it is not in the Queensberry rules."

"Then what method was it?"

"Kung Fu," Vulcan answered. "I learnt it when I was in China."

"I might have guessed it!"

"And so might I," Astara agreed. "I could hardly believe it when I saw William fall down almost before the fight began."

"I have had the opportunity of a 'foreign' education," Vulcan smiled.

"And so . . have I," Astara said.

"I know that now," he answered.

For a moment they looked into each other's eyes, then Astara thought they were being unkind to Lionel.

He loved her in his own way, and she knew what she would have felt if she had been forced to watch Vulcan holding another woman in his arms.

She got off his knees.

"I am sure my clothes will be dry by now," she said, "and I think we ought to go home."

"That is what we will do," Vulcan answered. "We will go home."

He accentuated the last word.

Astara went to Lionel's side.

"Thank you! Thank you for saving me . . but you have not told me yet how you . . knew where William would have . . taken me."

"I guessed he would have come here," Lionel answered. "It is one of the places he frequents with . . ."

He stopped suddenly as if he was going to say something indiscreet, and Astara knew there was no need to add any more. It was what she had suspected about "*The Kind Dragon*" in the first place.

"Thank you, dear Lionel," she said, "and although I love and admire Vulcan more than anyone else in the world, there will always be a place in my heart for you."

As she spoke she stood on tip-toe and kissed his cheek.

Then without waiting to see Lionel's confused gratification or what she suspected would be a scowl on Vulcan's face, she ran from the room.

. . . .

"Good-bye, dearest Uncle Roderick!" Astara said putting her arms round his neck. "We will write to you whenever it is possible and I will send you reports on all Vulcan's discoveries."

"Do that, and I will see they are copied and sent to the Association and the *Société*," Sir Roderick replied.

He turned to Vulcan and added:

"I was very impressed by those I read of your last trip when I was in Paris."

"You . . read Vulcan's reports?" Astara cried. "You never told me!"

"I had my reasons for not talking too much about Vulcan," Sir Roderick replied.

Astara looked at him a little anxiously.

"But you are . . glad I have . . married him now? You . . wanted me to be . . happy."

"I allowed you the judgement of love," Sir Roderick said, "and I promised that I would not prevent you giving the golden apple to the man of your choice."

"That is what Vulcan is," Astara said softly with a smile.

She looked up at the picture over the mantelpiece and taking her arms from Sir Roderick's neck, said:

"Do you realise, Uncle Roderick, that I have made exactly the same choice as Paris did?"

Sir Roderick raised his eye-brows and she explained:

"Hera, who is William, tried to bribe me with a great social position. Athene, who is Lionel, offered me the spoils of battle, but Paris chose Aphrodite. Do you remember why?"

She did not wait for him to reply, but went on:

"Aphrodite offered him nothing but love, and that is what Vulcan is . . giving me."

As if she could not help herself she put out her hand towards him. He took it and kissed it. Then he said:

"We should be on our way if we are to reach Dover before nightfall."

"I am ready."

Astara turned again to Sir Roderick.

"It will be so exciting to come back, Uncle Roderick, and see all the improvements you have made."

"Do not forget they are for you, my dear, and your husband."

"But not for many, many years. We have so many countries to explore, so many books to write and Vulcan has so many lectures to give."

She smiled radiantly, then she said in a different tone of voice:

"There is only one . . thing we thought we . . might do, Uncle Roderick, if you agree."

"What is that?" he enquired.

"We will not only send you and bring you back from time to time Vulcan's pictures and his books . . but we . . ."

Astara stopped and blushed a little, then she finished almost in a whisper:

". . we thought we . . might also . . leave any . . babies we happened to have with you until they were old enough to . . travel with . . us."

Sir Roderick looked at her incredulously, then he laughed.

"But of course!" he said. "I realise that they, like you and Vulcan, are now my responsibility. Well, the house is big enough. I am prepared to provide for as many as you like!"

Astara flung her arms around his neck.

"I thought you would say that, and it will make things so much easier."

"I see you are expecting me to live to a ripe old age, and still have my uses," Sir Roderick remarked, but his eyes were twinkling.

"You will certainly disappoint us if you do anything so stupid as to die," Vulcan remarked.

"Get off with you both!" Sir Roderick said. "I can see that my role in the future is going to be very different from what it was in the past – a nursemaid – an aged grandfather – oh, well, I have done everything else in my life so far. I might as well try that!"

He laughed again and with his arm round Astara he walked with them into the Hall.

Outside a Phaeton with a team of four chestnuts as magnificent as those which belonged to William was waiting.

The luggage in the charge of Chang had already gone ahead.

Astara looked at the horses with delight.

"Vulcan is thrilled with his wedding present!" she exclaimed, "but like a great many other things you will have to look after them until we return."

"That is what I intend to do," Sir Roderick replied, "and they will give you something to think about when you are riding a refractory mule!"

"I shall dream about them at night," Vulcan promised, "unless they make Astara jealous."

"I shall be, if you think or dream of anything except me," she said.

She put her hand in his as she spoke and they ran down the steps together and he helped her into the Phaeton.

"Good-bye, darling Uncle Roderick!" she cried. "Take care of yourself."

"That is what I am saying to you," he answered.

As he spoke Vulcan signalled to the grooms to let the horses go while one of them sprang up into the seat behind.

It was still early in the morning, but the sunshine glinted on the lake, on the trees, on the silver bridles of the horses, and the diamond ring on Astara's finger.

Sir Roderick watched until they were out of sight, then with a sigh he walked back into the house and across the Hall.

He did not go to the Salon but into the Library.

Standing on his desk was the miniature of Charlotte Beverley which along with several other things belonging to her mother Astara had left in his keeping.

Sir Roderick stood for a moment looking at the miniature, then he picked it up in his hands.

"Are you satisfied, Charlotte?" he asked. "I knew that Vulcan was exactly the man you would want as a son-in-law, and that Astara, like all your sex, would never be able to resist a man who ignored her!"

He smiled a little wistfully. Then as he put the miniature down again he added:

"I suppose you know, wherever you are, how much I still miss you! But now I shall be sharing your grandchildren with you, and that will be some consolation – to me at any rate."

As he finished speaking Sir Roderick walked from the desk to the window and stood looking out at the lake.

Golden in the sunshine it was the colour of Astara's hair, as it had been of her mother's.

Coming next in your collection of
The Romantic Novels of
BARBARA CARTLAND

LOVE IS INVINCIBLE

The Marquis of Shawforde, who has just inherited his title and ancestral estate, meets lovely Lucille Winterton out riding and falls in love.

The Marquis's family, however, learn of his infatuation, and as they want him to marry a Duke's daughter, they send for his uncle.

Lord Kenyon Shaw has just returned from India, where he has taken part in the powerful "Great Game".

This is a brilliant, very secret organisation which opposed the Russian infiltration of the North-West Frontier and their affiliation with the tribesmen.

Lord Kenyon travels to the country to save his nephew from a "designing woman", and mistakes her beautiful elder sister Delia for Lucille.

They quarrel, then Delia learns that he is in danger and saves him from the vengeful Russian spies.

How Delia nurses Lord Kenyon back to health, how the Marquis makes up his own mind, and how Lord Kenyon finds love is invincible is all told in this riveting new novel by Barbara Cartland.